BY PIERCE BROWN

Red Rising

Golden Son

Morning Star

Iron Gold

Dark Age

Light Bringer

IRON GOLD

SPECIAL SNEAK PREVIEW

IRON GOLD

SPECIAL SNEAK PREVIEW

PIERCE BROWN

DEL REY
NEW YORK

Published in the United States by Del Rey, an imprint of Random House, a division of Penguin Random House LLC, New York.

Del Rey and the Circle colophon are registered trademarks of Penguin Random House LLC.

Printed in the United States of America on acid-free paper

randomhousebooks.com

7th Printing

First Edition

For the Howlers

In the tenth year of the Solar War

Commissioned by Sovereign Virginia au Augustus, 753 PCE

WHITE FLEET

MERCURY

VENUS DOCKYARDS

VENUS

ASH LORD'S FLEET

EARTH

LUNA

HOME GUARD

SOCIETY REMNANT

Planets controlled by the Ash Lord

SOLAR REPUBLIC

Spheres liberated by the Republic

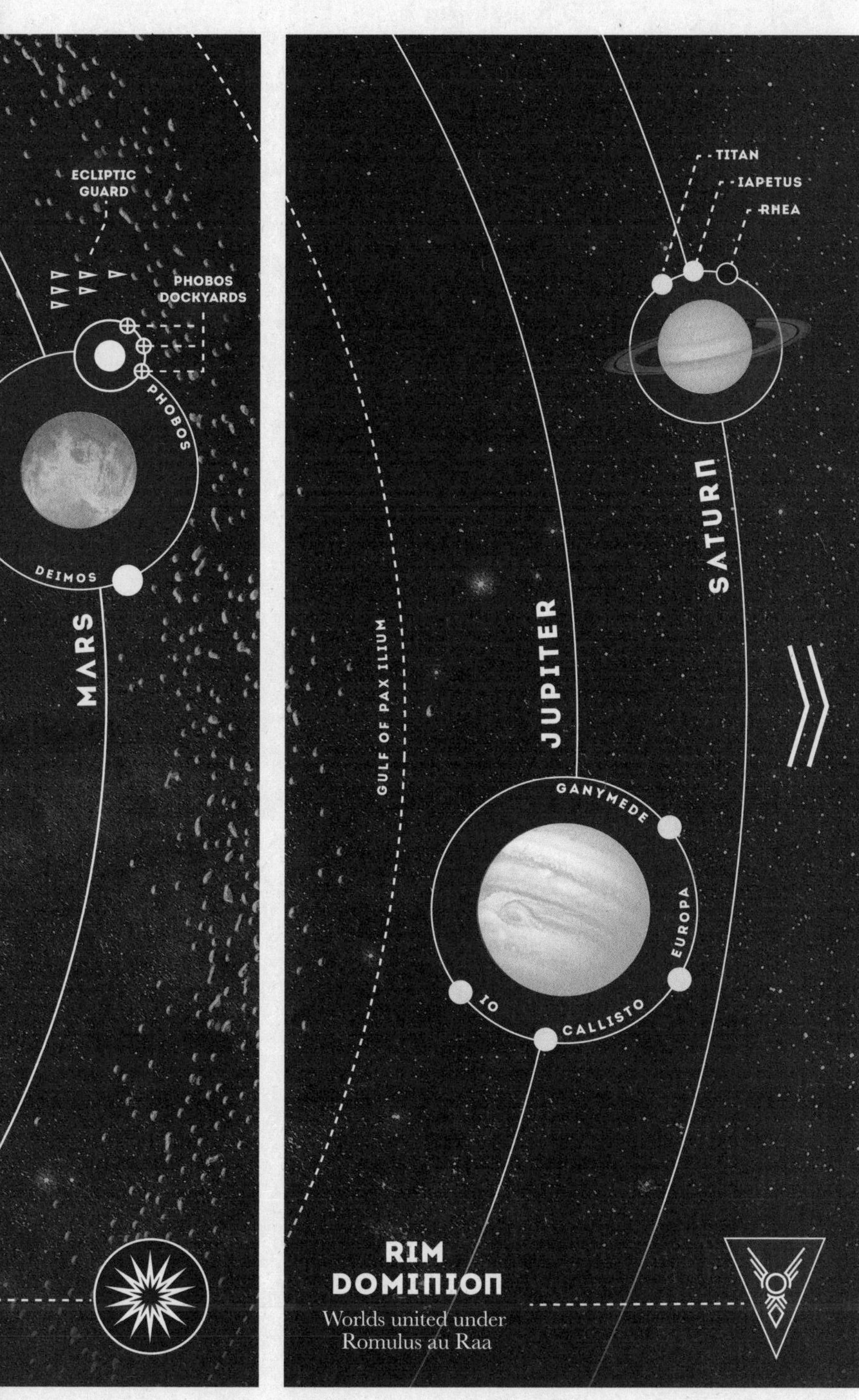
ECLIPTIC GUARD
PHOBOS DOCKYARDS
PHOBOS
DEIMOS
MARS
GULF OF PAX ILIUM
JUPITER
GANYMEDE
EUROPA
CALLISTO
IO
TITAN
IAPETUS
RHEA
SATURN
RIM DOMINION
Worlds united under Romulus au Raa

DRAMATIS PERSONAE

REDS

DARROW OF LYKOS/THE REAPER ArchImperator of the Republic, husband to Virginia

RHONNA Niece of Darrow

LYRIA OF LAGALOS A Gamma Red

DANCER, SENATOR O'FARAN Senator of the Republic, Ares lieutenant

DANO Colleague of Ephraim

GOLDS

VIRGINIA AU AUGUSTUS/MUSTANG Reigning Sovereign of the Republic, wife to Darrow, mother to Pax

PAX Son of Darrow and Virginia

Magnus au Grimmus/the Ash Lord   Former ArchImperator to Octavia

Atalantia au Grimmus   Daughter of the Ash Lord

Cassius au Bellona   Former Morning Knight, guardian to Lysander

Lysander au Lune   Grandson of former Sovereign Octavia, heir to House Lune

Sevro au Barca/the Goblin   Howler, husband to Victra

Victra au Barca   Wife to Sevro, née Victra au Julii

Electra au Barca   Daughter of Sevro and Victra

Kavax au Telemanus   Head of House Telemanus, father to Daxo

Niobe au Telemanus   Wife to Kavax

Daxo au Telemanus   Heir and son of Kavax

Thraxa au Telemanus   Daughter of Kavax and Niobe

Romulus au Raa   Head of House Raa, Lord of the Dust, Sovereign of the Rim Dominion

Dido au Raa   Wife to Romulus, née Dido au Saud

Seraphina au Raa   Daughter of Romulus and Dido

Diomedes au Raa/the Storm Knight   Son of Romulus and Dido

Marius au Raa   Quaestor, son of Romulus and Dido

Apollonius au Valii-Rath/the Minotaur   Heir to House Valii-Rath

THARSUS AU VALII-RATH   Brother to Apollonius

ALEXANDAR AU ARCOS   Eldest grandson of Lorn

VANDROS   a Howler

CLOWN   a Howler

PEBBLE   a Howler

OTHER COLORS

HOLIDAY TI NAKAMURA   Legionnaire, sister to Trigg, a Gray

EPHRAIM TI HORN   Freelancer, former Son of Ares

SEFI   Queen of the Valkyrie, sister to Ragnar, an Obsidian

WULFGAR THE WHITETOOTH   ArchWarden of the Republic, an Obsidian

VOLGA FJORGAN   Colleague of Ephraim, an Obsidian

QUICKSILVER/REGULUS AG SUN   Richest man in the Republic, a Silver

PYTHA   Blue pilot, companion to Cassius and Lysander

CYRA SI LAMENSIS   Locksmith, colleague of Ephraim, a Green

PUBLIUS CU CARAVAL   The Copper Tribune, leader of the Copper bloc, a Copper

MICKEY   Carver, a Violet

THE FALL OF MERCURY

THE FURY

SILENT, SHE WAITS FOR the sky to fall, standing upon an island of volcanic rock amidst a black sea. The long moonless night yawns before her. The only sounds, a flapping banner of war held in her lover's hand and the warm waves that kiss her steel boots. Her heart is heavy. Her spirit wild. Peerless knights tower behind her. Salt spray beads on their family crests—emerald centaurs, screaming eagles, gold sphinxes, and the crowned skull of her father's grim house. Her Golden eyes look to the heavens. Waiting. The water heaves in. Out. The heartbeat of her silence.

THE CITY

Tyche, the jewel of Mercury, hunches in fear between the mountains and the sun. Her famed glass and limestone spires are dark. The Ancestor Bridge is empty. Here, Lorn au Arcos wept as a young man when he saw the messenger planet at sunset for the first time. Now, trash rolls through her streets, pushed by salty summer wind. Gone are the calls of the fishmongers at the wharf. Gone are the patter of pedestrian feet on the cobbles and the rumble of aircars and the laughter of the lowColor children who jump from the bridges into the waves on scorching summer days when the Trasmian sea winds are still. The city is quiet, its wealthy already gone to desert mountain retreats or government bunkers, its soldiers on its rooftops watching the sky, its poor having left for the desert or upon cramped boats destined for the Ismere Islands.

But the city is not empty.

Huddled masses fill the public transit systems that wend beneath the waves. And in the upstairs window of a tenement complex on the ugly fringes of the city, far from the water, where the working poor are kept, a little girl with Orange eyes fogs the window with her breath. The night sky sparks. Flashing and flaring with spurts of light like the fireworks her brother sometimes buys at the corner shop. She's been told there is a battle between big fleets high up there. She has never seen a starship. Her mother lies sick in the bedroom, unable to travel. Her father, who builds parts for engines, sits at the little plastic dinner table with his sons, knowing he cannot protect them. The holoCan washes them in pale light. Government news programs tell them to seek shelter. In her pocket the girl carries a folded piece of paper that she found in the gutter. On it is a little curved sword. She's seen it before on the cube. Her teachers at the government school say it brings chaos. War. It has set the spheres on fire. But now she secretly draws the blade in the fog her breath has made on the window, and she feels brave.

Then the bombs begin to fall.

THE BOMBS

They come from high-orbit Thor-class bombers piloted by farmboys from Earth and miners from Mars of the Twelfth Sunshine Squadron. Curses and prayers and tribal dragons and curved scythes have been sprayed upon them in aerosol paint. They dip through the clouds and fall over the sea, outracing their own sound. Their guidance chips are made by freeColors on Phobos. Their steel is mined and smelted by entrepreneurs in the Belt. Their ion propulsion engines are stamped with the winged heel of a company that makes consumer electronics and toiletries and weapons. Down and down they go to race shadowless over the desert, then the sea, carrying the weight of the newest empire under the sun.

The first bomb destroys the Hall of Justice on Tyche's Vespasian Island. Then it burrows a hundred meters into the earth before detonating against the bunker buried there, killing all inside. The second lands in the sea, fifteen kilometers from a fleet of refugees, where it sinks a Society warship, hiding under the chop. The third races over a spine of mountains north of Tyche when it is struck with a railgun round fired from a defense installation by a Gray teenager with acne scars and the charm of a sweetheart around his neck. It careens off its course and sputters across the sky before falling to the earth.

It detonates on the fringes of the city, far from the water, where it turns four blocks of tenement housing to dust.

THE REAPER

Silent, he lies encased in mankilling metal in the belly of a starship called the *Morning Star*. The fear swallows him now as it has done time and time before. The only sound is the whir of his armor's air filtration unit and the radio chatter of distant men and women. Around him lie his friends, they too cocooned in metal. Waiting. Eyes Red and Gold and Gray and Obsidian. Wolfheads mark their pauldrons. Tattoos their necks and arms. Wild empire breakers from Mars and Luna and Earth. Beyond them fly ships with names like *Spirit of Lykos, Hope of Tinos,* and *Echo of Ragnar.* They are painted white and led by a woman with onyx-dark skin. The Lion Sovereign said the white was for spring. For a new beginning. But the ships are stained. Smeared with char and patched wounds and mismatched panels. They broke the Sword Armada and the martyr Fabii. They conquered the heart of the Gold empire. They battled back the Ash Lord to the Core and have kept the dragons of the Rim at bay.

How could they ever stay clean?

Alone in his armor, waiting to fall from the sky, he remembers the girl who began it all. He remembers how her Red hair fell over her eyes. How her mouth danced with laughter. How she breathed as she lay atop him, so warm and fragile in a world far too cold. She has been dead longer than she was ever alive. And now that her dream has spread, he wonders if she would recognize it. And he wonders too if he were to die today, would he recognize the echo of his own life? What sort of man would his son become in this world he has made? He thinks of his son's face and how soon he will become a man. And he thinks of his Golden wife. How she stood on the landing pad, looking up at him, wondering if he'd ever return home again.

More than anything, he wants this to end.

Then the machine takes hold.

He feels the tug on his body. The pounding of his heart. The mad cackling of the Goblin and the howls of his friends as they try to forget their children, their loves, and be brave. Nausea in his gut rises as the magnetic rails charge behind him. With a shudder of metal, they fire him forward through the launch tube out into silent space at six times the speed of sound.

Men call him father, liberator, warlord, Slave King, Reaper. But he feels a boy as he falls toward the war-torn planet, his armor red, his army vast, his heart heavy.

It is the tenth year of war and the thirty-third of his life.

PART I

WIND

There is a poor, blind Samson in this land,
Shorn of his strength and bound in bonds of steel,
Who may, in some grim revel, raise his hand,
And shake the pillars of this Commonweal,
Till the vast Temple of our liberties
A shapeless mass of wreck and rubbish lies.

—Henry Wadsworth Longfellow

1

DARROW

Hero of the Republic

WEARY, I WALK UPON FLOWERS at the head of an army. Petals carpet the last of the stone road before me. Thrown by children from windows, they twirl lazily down from the steel towers that grow to either side of the Luna boulevard. In the sky, the sun dies its slow, weeklong death, staining the tattered clouds and gathered crowd in bloody hues. Waves of humanity lap against security barricades, pressing inward on our parade as Hyperion City Watchmen in gray uniforms and cyan berets guard the route, shoving drunken revelers back into the crowd. Behind them, antiterrorism units prowl up and down the pavement, their fly-eyed goggles scanning irises, hands resting on energy weapons.

My own eyes rove the crowd.

After ten years of war, I no longer believe in moments of peace.

It's a sea of Colors that line the twelve-kilometer Via Triumphia. Built by my people, the Red slaves of the Golds, hundreds of years ago, the Triumphia is the avenue by which the Conquerors who tamed Earth held their own processions as they claimed continent after continent. Iron-spined murderers with eyes of gold and haughty menace once consecrated these same stones. Now, nearly a millennium later, we sully the Triumphia's sacred white marble by honoring Liberators with eyes of jet and ash and rust and soil.

Once, this would have filled me with pride. Jubilant crowds celebrating the Free Legions returned from vanquishing yet another threat to our fledgling Republic. But today I see holosigns of my head with a bloody crown atop it, hear the jeers from the Vox Populi as they wave banners emblazoned with their upside-down pyramid, and feel nothing but the weight of an endless war and a desperate longing to be once again in the embrace of my family. It has been a year since I've seen my wife and son. After the long voyage back from Mercury, all I want is to be with them, to fall into a bed, and to sleep for a dreamless month.

The last of my journey home lies before me. As the Triumphia widens and abuts the stairs that lead up to the New Forum, I face one final summit.

Faces drunk on jubilation and new commercial spirits gape up at me as I reach the stairs. Hands sticky with sweets wave in the air. And tongues, loose from those same commercial spirits and delights, cry out, shouting my name, or cursing it. Not the name my mother gave me, but the name my deeds have built. The name the fallen Peerless Scarred now whisper as a curse.

"Reaper, Reaper, Reaper," they cry, not in unison, but in frenzy. The clamor suffocates, squeezing with a billion-fingered hand: all the hopes, all the dreams, all the pain constricting around me. But so close to the end, I can put one foot after the other. I begin to climb the stairs.

Clunk.

My metal boots grind on stone with the weight of loss: Eo, Ragnar, Fitchner, and all the others who've fought and fallen at my side while somehow I have remained alive.

I am tall and broad. Thicker at my age of thirty-three than I was in my youth. Stronger and more brutal in my build and movement. Born Red, made Gold, I have kept what Mickey the Carver gave me. These Gold eyes and hair feel more my own than those of that boy who lived in the mines of Lykos. That boy grew, loved, and dug the earth, but he lost so much it often feels like it happened to another soul.

Clunk. Another step.

Sometimes I fear that this war is killing that boy inside. I ache to remember him, his raw, pure heart. To forget this city moon, this Solar War, and return to the bosom of the planet that gave birth to me before the boy inside is dead forever. Before my son loses the chance to ever know him. But the worlds, it seems, have plans of their own.

Clunk.

I feel the weight of the chaos I've unleashed: famines and genocide on Mars, Obsidian piracy in the Belt, terrorism, radiation sickness and disease spreading through the lower reaches of Luna, and the two hundred million lives lost in my war.

I force a smile. Today is our fourth Liberation Day. After two years of siege, Mercury has joined the free worlds of Luna, Earth, and Mars. Bars stand open. War-weary citizens rove the streets, looking for reason to celebrate. Fireworks crackle and blaze across the sky, shot from the roofs of skyscraper and tenement complex alike.

With our victory on the first planet from the sun, the Ash Lord has been pushed back to his last bastion, the fortress planet Venus, where his battered fleet guards precious docks and the remaining loyalists. I have come home to convince the Senate to requisition ships and men of the war-impoverished Republic for one final campaign. One last push on Venus to put this bloodydamn war to rest. So I can set down the sword and go home to my family for good.

Clunk.

I take a moment to glance behind me. Waiting at the foot of the stairs is my Seventh Legion, or the remnants of it. Twenty-eight thousand men and women where once there were fifty. They stand in casual order around a fourteen-pointed ivory star with a pegasus galloping at its center—held aloft by the famous Thraxa au Telemanus. The Hammer. After losing her left arm to Atalantia au Grimmus's razor, she had it replaced by a metal prototype appendage from Sun

Industries. Wild gold hair flutters behind her head, garlanded with white feathers given to her by Obsidian admirers.

In her mid-thirties, a stout woman with thighs thick as water drums and a freckled, bluff face. She grins past the shoulders of the Obsidians and Golds around her. Blue and Red and Orange pilots wave to the crowd. Red, Gray, and Brown infantry smile and laugh as pretty young Pinks and Reds duck under barriers and rush to drape necklaces of flowers around their necks, push bottles of liquor into their hands and kisses onto their mouths. They are the only full legion in today's parade. The rest remain on Mercury with Orion and Harnassus, battling with the Ash Lord's legions stranded there when his fleet retreated.

Clunk.

"Remember, you are but mortal," Sevro's bored voice drawls in my ear as white-haired Wulfgar and the Republic Wardens descend to greet us midway up the Forum stairs. Sevro sniffs my neck and makes a noise of distaste. "By Jove. You wretch. Did you dip yourself in piss before the occasion?"

"It's cologne," I say. "Mustang bought it for me last Solstice."

He's quiet for a moment. "Is it made out of piss?"

I scowl back at him, wrinkling my nose at the heaviness of liquor on his breath, and eye the ragged wolfcloak he wears over his ceremonial armor. He claims he hasn't washed it since the Institute. "You're really lecturing me about stenches? Just shut up and behave like an Imperator," I say with a grin.

Snorting, Sevro drops back to where the legendary Obsidian, Sefi Volarus, stands in her customary silence. He feigns an air of domesticity, but next to the giant woman, he looks a little like some sort of gutter dog an alcoholic father might ill-advisedly bring home to play with the children—washed and rid of fleas, but still possessing that weird mania behind the eyes. Pinched, thin lipped, with a nose crooked as an old knifefighter's fingers. He eyes the crowd with resigned distaste.

Behind him lope the pack of mangy Howlers he brought with us to Mercury. My bodyguards, now drunk as gallants at a Lykos Laureltide. Stalwart Holiday walks at their center, the snub-nosed woman doing her best to keep them in line.

There used to be more of them. So many more.

I smile as Wulfgar descends the stairs to meet me. A favorite son of the Rising, the Obsidian is a tree root of a man, gnarled and narrow, armored all in pale blue. He's in his early forties. His face angular as a raptor's, his beard braided like that of his hero, Ragnar.

One of the Obsidians to fight alongside Ragnar at the walls of Agea, Wulfgar was with the Sons of Ares that freed me from the Jackal in Attica. Now ArchWarden of the Republic, he smiles down at me from the step above, his black eyes crinkling at the corners.

"Hail libertas," I say with a smile.

"Hail libertas," he echoes.

"Wulfgar. Fancy meeting you here. You missed the Rain," I say.

"You did not wait for me to return, did you?" Wulfgar clucks his tongue. "My children will ask where I was when the Rain fell upon Mercury, and you know what I will have to tell them?" He leans forward with a conspiratorial smile. "I was making night soil, wiping my ass when I heard Barca had taken Mount Caloris." He rumbles out a laugh.

"I told you not to leave," Sevro says. "You'd miss out on all the fun, I said. You should have seen the Ashies route. Trails of piss all the way to Venus. You'd have loved it." Sevro grins at the Obsidian. It was Sevro who put a razor in his hand in the river mud of Agea. Wulfgar has his own razor now. Its hilt made from the fang of an ice dragon from Earth's South Pole.

"My blade would have sung that day were I not summoned by the Senate," he says.

Sevro sneers. "That's right. You ran home like a good little dog."

"A dog? I am a servant of the People, my friend. As are we all." His eyes find me with mild accusation and I understand the true meaning to his words. Wulfgar is a believer, like all Wardens. Not in me, but in the Republic, in the principles for which it stands, and the orders that the Senate gives. Two days before the Iron Rain over Mercury, the Senate, led by my old friend Dancer, voted against my proposal. They told me to maintain the siege. To not waste men, resources, on an assault.

I disobeyed and let the Rain fall.

Now a million of my men lie in the sands of Mercury and we have our Liberation Day.

Were Wulfgar with me on Mercury, he would not have joined our Rain against the Senate's permission. In fact, he might have tried to stop me. He's one of the few men alive who might manage. For a spell at least.

He spares a nod for Sefi. *"Njar ga hae, svester."* A rough translation is "Respect to you, sister" in *nagal.*

"Njar ga hir, bruder," she replies. No love lost between them. They have different priorities.

"Your weapons." Wulfgar gestures to my razor.

Sefi and I hand his Wardens our weapons. Muttering under his breath, Sevro hands over his as well. "Did you forget your toothpick?" Wulfgar asks, looking at Sevro's left boot.

"Treasonous yeti," Sevro mutters, and pulls a wicked blade long as a baby's body from his boot. The Warden who takes it looks terrified.

"Odin's fortune with the togas, Darrow," Wulfgar says to me as he motions for us to continue upward. "You will need it."

Arrayed at the top of the steps of the New Forum are the 140 Senators of the Republic. Ten per Color, all draped in white togas that flutter in the breeze. They peer down at me like a row of haughty pigeons on a wire. Red and Gold, mortal enemies in the Senate, bookend the row to either side. Dancer is missing. But I have eyes only for the lonely bird of prey that stands at the center of all the silly, vain, power-hungry little pigeons.

Her golden hair is bound tight behind her head. Her tunic is pure white, without the ribbons of their Color the others wear. And in her hand, she carries the Dawn Scepter—now a multi-hued gold baton half a meter long, with the pyramid of the Society recast into the fourteen-pointed star of the Republic at its tip. Her face is elegant and distant. A small nose, piercing eyes behind thick eyelashes, and a mischievous cat's smile growing on her face. The Sovereign of our Republic. Here at the summit of the stairs, her eyes shed the weight from my shoulders, the fear from my heart that I would never see her again. Through war and space and this damnable parade, I have traveled to find her again, my life, my love, my home.

I bend to my knee and look up into the eyes of the mother of my child.

"'Lo, wife," I say with a smile.

"'Lo, husband. Welcome home."

2

DARROW

Father

SILENE MANOR, THE SOVEREIGN's traditional Luna country retreat, is nestled five hundred kilometers north of Hyperion at the base of the Atlas Mountains on a small lake. The northern hemisphere of the moon, comprised of mountains and seas, is less populous than the belt of cities that girdle the equator. Though Mustang governs from the Palace of Light in the Citadel, Silene is the true home of my family, at least until we return to Mars. Built to resemble one of the papal villas on Earth's Lake Como, the stone house sits along the edge of a rocky cove, and spills down to the lake by means of switchbacked stairs cut into the rock.

Here the thin conifers whisper to heights four times those possible on Earth. They sway nearly two hundred meters in the air around the raised concrete landing pad where the steward of House Augustus, Cedric cu Platuu, waits with my wife's Lionguards as our shuttle lands. The small Copper greets Sevro and me with great alacrity, bowing deeply and flourishing his hand. Thraxa runs past him without even a greeting, eager to find her mother.

"ArchImperator," he gushes, plump cheeks flushing with delight. He's a short but ample man, built a bit like a plum with knobby arms and legs added as an afterthought. A whisper of a mustache, nearly as thin as the graying copper hair upon his head, wavers in the wind. "What gladness to see you again!"

"Cedric," I say, greeting the short man warmly. "I hear you've just had a birthday."

"Yes, my lord! My seventy-first. Though I do maintain one should stop counting after sixty."

"Prime work," Sevro says. "You look positively prepubescent."

"Thank you, my lord!"

Few know the secrets of the Citadel as well as Cedric; he was one of the gems of the Sovereign's court. Mustang, having thought highly of him during her time with Octavia, saw no need to dismiss a man so knowledgeable and dedicated to his duty.

"Where's the welcoming party?" Sevro asks, looking for his wife, Victra. Mustang and Daxo remained behind in Hyperion to deal with their unruly Senate, but promised to rejoin by dinnertime.

"Oh, the children are recently returned from a three-day adventure," Cedric says. "The Lady Telemanus took them to the ruins of the USS *Davy Crockett* in the Atlas Mountains. Merrywater's own! I hear they had quite a time around that old wreck. Quite. A. Time, yes. Learned many lessons and expanded their individual initiative. As your curriculum requested, *dominu—*" Cedric's eyes nearly pop out of his head before he corrects himself. "As your curriculum requested, *sir.*"

"Is my wife here yet?" Sevro asks gruffly.

"Not yet, sir. Her valet said she would be late to dinner. I believe there were labor strikes in her warehouses in Endymion and Echo City. It's all over the holoNews."

"She didn't even show to the Triumph," Sevro mutters. "I looked fabulous."

"She has missed you at your most prime, sir."

"Right. See, Darrow? Cedric agrees." What he hasn't noticed is Cedric shuffling away from the odious stench of his wolfcloak.

"Cedric, where is my son?" I ask the man.

He smiles. "I think you can guess, sir."

The sounds of neoPlast swords knocking together and boots on stone greet Sevro and me as we enter the dueling grotto. There, vines crawl over granite fountains and along the damp stone floor. Evergreen needles drift in cumulous shapes from the top of the trees. And in the center of the grotto, under the watching eyes of the gargoyles adorning the fountains, a young boy and girl circle each other at the center of a chalk circle. The seven other children of their pack watch on, along with two Gold women. Sevro pulls me to the side so we remain unseen and sit out of sight on the edge of a granite fountain to watch.

The boy at the center of the circle is ten, lean and proud. He laughs like his mother and broods like his father. His hair is the color of straw, his face round and flushed with youth. Rose-gold eyes burn from under long lashes. He's larger than I remember, older, and it feels so impossible that he could have come from me. That he could have thoughts of his own. That he'll love, smile, die like the rest of us.

His brow is furrowed now in concentration. Sweat pours down his face, matting his hair as his opponent strikes his knee a glancing blow.

The girl is nine and narrow-faced like a sleek hunting dog. Electra, the eldest of Sevro's three daughters, is taller than my son and twice as thin. But while Pax radiates an inner joy that makes adults' eyes twinkle, there's a deep grimness to the girl. Her eyes are dusky gold and hidden behind heavy lids. Sometimes when they look at me, I feel them judging with an aloofness that reminds me of her mother.

Sevro leans forward eagerly. "I'll wager Aja's razor against Apollonius's helm that my wee monster beats the piss out of your boy."

"I'm not going to bet on our children," I whisper in indignation.

"I'll throw Aja's Institute ring in as well."

"Have some decency, Sevro. They're our children."

"And Octavia's cape."

"I want the Falthe Ivory Tree."

Sevro gasps. "I love the Ivory Tree. Where else will I hang my trophies?"

I shrug. "No Ivory Tree, no bet."

"Bloodydamn savage," he says, sticking out a hand to shake. "You have a deal." Sevro's become quite the collector—acquiring a hoard of trophies from Gold Imperators, knights, and would-be kings. He hangs their rings and weapons and crests from the boughs of the ivory tree he uprooted from the House Falthe compound on Earth and moved to his home on Luna.

We watch as Electra redoubles her onslaught against Pax. My son continues to back away, to sidestep, allowing her to overextend. Once she does, he twirls his plastic razor toward her rib cage. It connects lightly. "Point!" he shouts.

"I'm counting, Pax. Not you," Niobe au Telemanus says. Kavax's wife is a serene woman with a bird's nest of untamable graying hair and skin the color of cherrywood. The tribal tattoos of her Pacific Islander ancestors cover her arms. "Three to two, for Pax."

"Mind your balance, and stop overextending, Electra," says Thraxa. "You'll lose your footing if you're on an unstable surface, like a ship deck or ice." She sits on the edge of a fountain, miraculously already having found a bottle of beer.

Brow furrowed in anger, Electra rushes Pax again. They move fast for children, but since they're still shy of puberty, their movements are not yet graceful. Electra feints high, then twists her wrist to slash savagely down, hitting Pax's shoulder. "Point for Electra," Niobe says. Sevro has to stop himself from clapping. Pax tries to recover, but Electra is on him. Three more quick blows knock his razor from his hand. He falls down and Electra lifts her razor to smash him hard on the head.

Thraxa slips forward and catches the blade mid-swing with her metal hand. "Temper, temper, little lady." She pours a little beer on her head.

Electra glares up at her.

Sevro can't contain himself any longer. "My little harpy!" He lunges up off the bench and I follow through to the grotto. "Daddy's home!" A smile slashes across Electra's dour face as she turns to see her father. She runs to him and lets him scoop her up off the ground. Looks rather like he's hugging a limp fish. Some of the children flinch back when they see Sevro. And when they see me emerge from behind the vines, they stiffen and bow with perfect manners. Not one born since the fall of House Lune has the sigils implanted on their hands.

We raise them in packs of nine now, setting children of disparate

Colors together early in their schooling with hopes of creating the bonds that I found at the Institute, but without the murder and starvation. Pax's best friend, Baldur, a quiet gap-toothed Obsidian boy who is already nearly as tall as Sevro, helps Pax up. He tries to dust Pax off before Pax shoos him away and looks over at us.

I expected him to rush to me like Electra, but he doesn't. And in that moment, a very sharp spasm of pain goes through the deeper part of me. When I left him, he was a boy, brimming with reckless life, but the hesitation, the coldness in him now, is from the world of men. Minding his pack, he walks forward very calmly and bows at the waist, no deeper than manners require. "Hello, Father."

"My boy," I say with a smile. "You've grown like a weed."

"That's what happens when you age," he says, an edge to his words. I always thought when I became a man, I'd feel more confident, but towering over this boy, I feel so very small. I lost my own father to a cause; have I doomed Pax to the same fate?

"He's not generally such a snot," Niobe says later as we stand to the side after the children are dismissed from the day's practice. Pax leaves quickly and in a mood. Baldur rushes to keep up.

"Take the angst as a compliment, Darrow," Thraxa mumbles. "He just misses his father. I felt the same way anytime the old man was away on one of Augustus's errands." She pulls a slim burner from her pocket and lights it in the coals of one of the copper braziers that line the crumbling walls of the grotto. Niobe plucks it from her fingers and puts it out on her daughter's metal arm.

"Was Daxo ever like that?" I ask.

"Daxo?" Niobe laughs. "Daxo was born stoic as a stone."

"Plotting in the womb from conception," Thraxa mutters, and sips her beer. "We used to make owl hoots at him. Always watching the rest of us out the window. Big brother never wanted to play our games. Only his own."

"And you were such a paragon?" Niobe asks. "You used to eat cow pies."

Thraxa shrugs. "Better than your cooking." She steps out of range of her mother's reach and lights a replacement burner. "Thank Jove we had Browns."

Niobe rolls her eyes and touches my arm. "The miscreant is right, Darrow. Pax just missed you. You've time to make up."

I smile at her but watch Sevro walking away toward the water with Electra. "You know you're Daddy's favorite, don't you?" he's saying to her. I fight back my jealousy. He always seems able to pick right back up where he left off with his family. I wish I had that same gift.

I seek my mother out in the garden that runs along the side of one of the stone storage sheds. She's hunched in the black dirt with two other Red servant women and a Red man, her bare feet sticking out behind her as she plants bulbs in the ground in tidy rows. I pause a moment at the edge of the garden to watch her, just as I used to watch from the stairwell in our little home in Lykos as she made her night tea. I was afraid of her after Father died. She was always quick with a swat or a barbed word. I thought I deserved the treatment. How much easier the love between us would have been if I'd known as a child that her anger and my fear came from a pain neither one of us deserved. The love in me wells up for her as I remember what she's endured, and for a brief flicker, I ache to see my father again. For him to see my mother free.

"Are you just going to watch like a wastrel or are you going to help us plant?" she asks without looking up.

"I'm not sure I'd be a good farmer," I say.

She stands with the help of one of her companions, dusts the dirt from her pants, and takes her time setting her tools away before coming to say hello. She's only eighteen years older than I am, but she wears the years hard. Still, she is stronger by leagues than when she lived below. Her joints are worn from years in the mines. But her cheeks are ruddy with life now. Our physicians have helped relieve most of the symptoms of the stroke and heart condition that ravaged her. I know she feels guilty for this life. This luxury, when my father and so many others wait for us in the Vale. Her work in the garden and on the grounds is a penance for surviving.

My mother gives me a hard hug. "My son." She breathes me in before pulling back to look all the way up to my face. "You put the death in me when I heard of that damn Iron Rain. You put the death in all of us."

"I'm sorry. They shouldn't have told you before that I was unaccounted for."

She nods and says nothing, and I realize how deep her worry went. How they must have huddled in the living room here or in the Citadel and listened to the holoNews just like everyone else. The Red man shuffles to join us, his bad leg dragging behind.

"'Lo, Dancer," I say past my mother. My old mentor wears laborer's garments instead of his senatorial robes. His hair is gray, his face fatherly and creased from hard years. But there's still mischief in his rebel eyes. "Given up the Senate for gardening, have you?"

"I'm a man of the people," he says with a shrug. "Good to have dirt under the nails again. The gardeners in that museum the Senate gave me won't let me touch a damn weed. 'Lo, Sevro."

"Politician," Sevro says, joining me from behind. Heedless of the mood, he pretends like he's going to scoop my mother up into the air, but she scowls at him and he turns the scoop into a gentle hug.

"Better," she says. "You nearly broke my hip the last time."

"Oh, don't be such a Pixie," he mutters.

"Say that again?"

He steps back. "Nothing, ma'am."

"What word from Leanna?" I ask.

"They're well. Was hoping to visit them soon. Maybe take Pax along to Icaria in the winter. This place gets too cold for these old bones."

"All the way to Mars?" I ask.

"It's his home," she says sharply. "You want him to forget where he came from? Red's as deep in his blood as Gold. Not that he's ever reminded it, 'cept by me."

Dancer looks away, as if to give us privacy.

"He'll go to Mars," I say. "We all will when it's safe."

We might control Mars, but that's a far cry from it being a world of harmony. The Sirenian continent is still infested by a Gold army of iron-skinned veterans, just like the battleground of South Pacifica on Earth. The Ash Lord hasn't risked putting a major fleet in orbit in years, but ground wars are decidedly more stubborn than their astral counterparts.

"And when will it be safe, according to you?" my mother asks.

"Soon."

Neither Dancer nor my mother is impressed by that answer. "And how long are you staying here?" she asks.

"A month, at least. Rhonna and Kieran will be coming, like you asked."

"About bloody time. Thought Mercury had stolen them."

"Victra and the girls will come up for a spell too. Though I do have business in Hyperion at the end of the week."

"With the Senate. Asking for more men." Her tone's as sour as her eyes.

I sigh and look at Dancer. "Infecting my mother with your politics now?"

He laughs. "Deanna most certainly has a mind of her own."

"With both of you in my ears I'll go deaf," she says.

"Plug your ears," Sevro replies. "It's what I do when they jabber about politics."

Dancer snorts. "If only your wife did the same."

"Careful, boyo. She's got ears everywhere. She could be listening now."

"Why weren't you at the Triumph?" I ask Dancer.

He grimaces. "Please. We both know I've got no stomach for pomp. Especially on this damn moon. Give me dirt and air and friends." He looks fondly at the trees around. A shadow passes over his face at the thought of returning to Hyperion. "But I must be heading back to the mechanized Babylon. Deanna, thank you for letting me garden with you. It's just what I needed."

"You're not staying for supper?" my mother asks.

"Unfortunately, there are other gardens that need tending. Speaking of which . . . Darrow, could I have a moment?"

Dancer and I leave my mother and Sevro bickering about the smell of his wolfcloak to walk along a dirt footpath leading into the trees toward the lake. A patrol skiff skims the water on the far shore. "How are you?" he asks me. "None of that patriotic hero shit. Remember, I know all your tells."

"Tired," I admit. "You'd think a month's journey back would let me catch up on sleep. But there's always something."

"*Can* you sleep?" he asks.

"Sometimes."

"Lucky bastard. I piss the bed," he admits. "Probably twice a month. I don't ever remember the bloodydamn dreams, but my body sure as hell does." He was in the thick of the fighting to free Mars. The tunnel wars there were even nastier than the block fighting on Luna. Even the Obsidians don't sing songs of their victories in the tunnels. The Rat War, they call it. Over the course of three years, Dancer personally liberated over a hundred mines with the Sons of Ares. If Fitchner is the father of the Rising, it'd be fair to call Dancer the favorite uncle, despite the dissolution of the Sons of Ares.

"You can take meds," I say. "Most of the vets do."

"*Psych meds?* I don't need Yellow synthetics. I'm a Red of Faran. My wits are damn sure more important than a dry bed." On that we agree. Even though he's my wife's main opposition in the Senate, and thereby mine, he's still as dear to me as my own family. Only when Mars and her moons were declared free did Dancer give up the gun and take up the senatorial toga to found the Vox Populi, the "Voice of the People," a socialist lowColor party to counter what he saw as undue Gold influence over the Republic. It's a bloodydamn thorn in my boots every time he gives a speech on proportional representation. If he had his way, there'd be five hundred lowColor senators to every Gold senator. Good math. Bad reality.

"Still, must be good to feel grass under your boots instead of sand and metal," he says softly. "Must be good to be home."

"It is." I hesitate and look out at the rocky shore below. "Gets harder every time. To come back. You'd think I look forward to it, but . . . I don't know. I dread it in a way. Every time Pax grows a centimeter, it feels like an indictment against me for not being there to see it." I pick a loose thread impatiently. "Not to mention the longer I spend here, the more time the Ash Lord has to prepare Venus, and the longer this all stretches out."

His face hardens at the mention of the war. "And how long do you think this will . . . stretch out?"

"That depends, doesn't it?" I ask. "You're the only thing standing in my way of getting the men I need to end this."

"That's always your answer. Isn't it? More men." He sighs. "I'm the mouth of the Vox Populi, not the brain."

"You know, Dancer, humility isn't always a virtue."

"You disobeyed the Senate," he says flatly. "We did not give you permission to launch an Iron Rain. We preached caution and—"

"I won, didn't I?"

"This isn't the Sons of Ares any longer, much as you and I both wish it were. Virginia and her Optimates were content to let you run roughshod over the Senate, but the people are learning just how strong their voice is." He steps close to me. "Still, they revere you."

"Not all of them."

"Please. You've got cults that say prayers in your name. Who else has that?"

"Ragnar." I hesitate. "And Lysander au Lune."

"The line of Silenius died with Octavia. You were a fool to let that boy go, but if he was alive we'd know it. He got swallowed up by the war just like the rest of them. That leaves only you. The people love you, Darrow. You can't abuse that love. Whatever you do, you set an example. So if you don't follow the law, why should our Imperators, our Governors? Why should anyone else? How are we supposed to govern if you go off and do whatever you damn well please, like you're a—" He catches himself.

"A Gold."

"You know what I mean. The Senate was elected. You were not."

"I do what's necessary. You and I always have. But the rest of them, they do what gets them reelected. Why should I listen to them?" I smile at him. "Maybe you want an apology. Will that get me the men I need?"

"It may be too late for apologies."

I raise an eyebrow. I wish I could say his coldness is alien to me, but that bond between us has never been the same since he learned how I bought my peace with Romulus. I gave Romulus the Sons of Ares. Those were Dancer's men I left to die on the Rim. The guilt I felt for that defined our relationship for years, made me desperate for his approval. I thought if I could destroy the Ash Lord, I could amend the horror I consigned those men and women to. Nothing has been amended. Nothing will be. And it breaks my heart to know Dancer will never love me again the way I love him.

"Are we threatening each other now, Dancer? Thought you and I were beyond that. We started this together."

"Aye. We did. I care for you as if you were my own blood. Have ever since you came to me covered in dirt, no taller than my nose. But even you have to follow the laws of the Republic you helped build. Because when the law is not obeyed, the ground is fertile for tyrants."

I sigh. "You've been reading again."

"Damn right. The Golds hoarded our history so they could pretend they owned it. It's my duty as a free man to read so I'm not blind, being led around by my nose."

"No one is leading you around by your nose."

He snorts his disagreement. "When I was a soldier, I watched as your wife gave pardons to murderers, to slavers, and I bore it because I was told it was necessary to win the war. I watch now as our people live fifteen to a room with scraps for food, rags for healthcare, while the highColor aristocracy live in towers, and I bear it because I'm told it is necessary to win the war. I'll be damned if I sit back and watch another tyrant replace the one we left behind because it is necessary to win the fucking war."

"Spare me the speeches, man. My wife's no tyrant. It was her idea to diminish the strength of the Sovereign in the New Compact. Her choice to give that strength to the Senate. She helped give our people a voice. You think that was convenient for her? You think that's what a tyrant would do?"

He fixes me with hard eyes. "I wasn't talking about her."

I see.

"I remember when you told me I was a good man who'd have to do bad things," I say. "Your stomach go soft? Or have you spent so much time with politicians that you've forgotten what the enemy looks like? Usually they're about seven foot tall, wear a big Pyramid badge, oh, and they've got Red blood all over their hands."

"And so do you," he says. "One million was the total loss, wasn't it? One million for Mercury. You might be willing to bear that. But the rest of us tire of the weight. I know the Obsidians do. I know I do."

"So that leaves us at an impasse."

"It does. You're my friend," he says, voice heavy with emotion. "You will always be my friend. I won't put a dagger in your back. But I will stand up to you. I will do what is right."

"And so will I." I put out my hand. He takes it and lingers for a moment before walking down the path. He turns before it bends into the trees. "Is there something you're not telling me, Darrow? If there is, now is the time. When it's between just us friends."

"I've no secrets from you," I say, wishing it were true, wishing he believed me. Wishing he were still the leader of the Sons of Ares, so we could bear our secrets together like we once did. Sadly, not all adversaries are enemies.

He turns and limps back to the garden to say farewell to my mother. They embrace and he makes his way to the southern landing pads where his Warden escorts wait. He takes a white wool toga from one and puts it on over his shirt before he goes up the ramp.

"What did he want?" Sevro asks.

"What do all politicians want?"

"Prostitutes."

"Control."

"He knows about the emissaries?"

"He couldn't."

Sevro watches Dancer's wool toga billow in the wind as he boards his shuttle. "I liked the bastard better in armor."

"So did I."

3

DARROW

The Fantasy

DINNER IS SERVED SHORTLY AFTER Daxo and Mustang arrive from Hyperion with my brother Kieran and niece, Rhonna. We eat at a long wooden table covered with candles and hearty provincial Martian dishes spiced with curry and cardamom. Sevro, swarmed by his daughters, makes faces at them as they eat. But when the air cracks with a sonic boom, he bolts upright, looks at the sky, and runs off into the house, urging his children to stay put. He returns a whole half an hour later arm in arm with his wife, hair a mess, two jacket buttons missing, touching a white napkin to a bloodied, split lip. My old friend Victra, immaculate in a high-collared green jacket threaded with gemstones, beams devilishly across the patio at me. She's seven months pregnant with their fourth daughter. "Well, if it isn't the Reaper in the leathery flesh. Apologies, my goodman. I'm dreadfully late."

Her long legs cover the distance in three strides.

I greet her with a hug. She squeezes my butt hard enough to make me jump. She kisses Mustang on the head and slides into a chair, dominating the table. "Hello, gloomy one," she says to Electra. She looks at young Pax and Baldur, who've been huddled conspiratorially at the far end of the table. Both boys blush furiously. "Will one of you handsome lads pour Aunty Victra some juice? She's had a hellish day." They scramble over one another to be the first to grab the pitcher. Baldur wins, and, pleased as a peacock, the quiet Obsidian lad solemnly pours Victra a towering glass. "Damnable mechanics union is on strike again. I've got docks full of freight that's ready to move, but the little bastards got all spiced up by a Vox Populi mouthpiece and took the power couplings out of more than half the ships in my Luna food haulers and hid them."

"What do they want?" Mustang asks.

"Aside from the moon to starve? Higher wages, better living conditions . . . the usual tripe. They say it's too expensive to live on Luna with their wages. Well, there's plenty of room on Earth!"

"How ungrateful of the unwashed peasants," my mother says.

"I detect your sarcasm, Deanna, and I'm choosing to ignore it in honor of our recently returned heroes. There will be enough debate later in the week. Anyway, I'm practically a saint. Mother would have sent Grays in to crack their ungrateful skulls. Thank Jove the tinmen still bloody any Vox they see."

"It's their right to bargain collectively," Mustang says, reaching down to wipe a bit of hummus off the face of Sevro's youngest, Diana. "Written in ink in the New Compact."

"Yes, of course it is. Unions are the heart of fair labor," Victra mutters. "It's the only thing Quicksilver and I agree upon."

Mustang smiles. "Better. You're a paragon of the Republic once again."

"You only just missed Dancer," Sevro says.

"I thought it reeked of self-righteousness." Victra goes to sip her juice and jumps in surprise. Baldur still stands at her side, smiling a bit too earnestly. "Oh, you're still here. Begone, creature." She kisses her fingers and then presses them to Baldur's cheek, pushing him away. He goes, drifting on air back to my envious son.

Afterwards, as the children go off into the vineyard to play, we retire to the back grotto. My family, those by blood and by choice, surround me. For the first time in over a year, I feel peace settling into me. My wife puts her feet in my lap and instructs me to rub them.

"I think Pax is in love with you, Victra," Mustang laughs as Daxo pours her a glass of wine. His hands dwarf the bottle. A taller man than I am, he has difficulty sitting in his chair and keeps accidentally kicking my shins under the table. Kieran and his wife, Dio, hold hands on a bench by the fire. When I was younger, I remember thinking how much she looked like Eo. But now, as time passes, the shadow of my wife's face fades and I see only the woman who is the center of my brother's being. She lurches forward suddenly, away from a shower of embers as Niobe dumps another log on the flames. Thraxa sits off in the corner, furtively lighting a burner.

"Well, Pax could have worse an idol than his godmother," Victra says, eyeing her husband, who is picking his teeth with a splinter of wood he's pried from the outdoor table. She pushes him with her foot. "That's grotesque. Stop."

"Sorry."

"Yet you're not stopping."

"Bit of gristle, my love." He turns like he's throwing the splinter away, but keeps picking. "Got it," he says gloomily. Instead of throwing the salvaged gristle to the side, he chews on it and swallows. "Beef."

"Beef?" Mustang looks back at the table. "We had chicken and lamb."

Sevro frowns. "Odd. Kieran, when did we last have beef?"

"At the Howler dinner, three days ago." Noses wrinkle around the table.

Sevro chuckles to himself. "Then it was well aged."

Daxo shakes his head and continues sketching angels for Diana, who sits on his lap admiring the man's work. He's no fool with a razor, but his true art is made with a stylus. Victra looks helplessly at Mustang over her juice, despairing of her husband. "Proof, my dear, that love is blind."

"Mickey can fix that face if you're tired of looking at it," I say.

"Good luck. You'd have to pry the decadent sprite away from his laboratory," Daxo says. The bald man considers Diana's addition of a cruelly barbed trident to the angel he's drawn. "Not to mention his admirers. He brought quite the menagerie to the Opera last September. It was a bit like a Hieronymus Bosch painting come alive. One of them was even an actress. Can you imagine?" he asks Mustang. "Your father would have chewed through his cheek to see lowColors sitting in the Elorian."

"He's not the only one," Victra says. "Too much new money these days. Quicksilver's friends." She shivers.

"Well, money doesn't buy culture, does it?" Daxo replies.

"Not at all, my goodman. Not at all."

As the night deepens, the orange fingers of the slow sunset thread their way through the trees. I let go of the strain in my shoulders and sink deeper into my cup, listening to my friends chatter and joke while little blue bugs flicker and stab violent light into the late summer twilight. The trees rustle beyond the terrace; the shouts of children come from the grounds as they play night games. The blistering sand seas of Mercury seem so far away now. The stench of war so remotc in my mind thcy arc littlc morc than shards of half-forgotten dreams.

This is how life should be.

This peace. This laughter.

But even now I feel it slipping through my fingers like that faraway sand. I sense the House Augustus Lionguards out in the darkness of the forest, watching the sky, the shadows, helping us stay inside the fantasy a moment longer. Mustang catches my eye and nods toward the door.

Forcing myself to part ways from my friends as the Telemanuses give a rousing, drunken rendition of their family's song, "The Fox of Summerfall," I follow several minutes after Mustang disappears into the main house. The manor halls here are older even than those of the Citadel of Light. History is the mortar of the place. Relics from older ages adorn walls, festoon shelves. Octavia called this place home as a child. Her essence lingers in the rafters and the attic and the gardens, as do those of her ancestors and child. It is where Lysander would have played long before his path crossed mine. I feel the imprint the Lunes have left on the home. At first I thought it strange living in the house of my greatest enemy, but in all humanity, who knew the burdens Mustang and I face as well as Octavia? In life, I loathed her. In death, I understand her.

The scent of my wife reaches me before the sight of her. Our room is warm and the door shudders shut behind me on a rusted metal latch. A bottle of wine is open on the table beside the fireplace, where eagles and crescent moons of House Lune are carved into the stone corbels. Mustang's slippers lie discarded on the floor. The ring of her father and my House Mars ring rest on the table beside her datapad, which flashes away with new messages.

She's spooled herself into a chair on our veranda like a bit of golden yarn, reading the dog-eared book of Shelley's poetry Roque gave her years ago during their summer of opera and art in Agea, after the Institute. She doesn't look up as I approach. I stand behind her, considering better of speaking, and slide a hand through her hair. I knead my thumbs into the muscles of her neck and back. Her proud shoulders relent against my fingers and she turns her book over in her lap. Sharing a life threads more than flesh and blood together. It weaves her memories in and around and through mine.

The more I know of her, the more I share of her, the more I love her in a way the boy I used to be never knew how to love. Eo was a flame, dancing against the wind. I tried to catch her. Tried to hold her. But she was never meant to be held.

My wife is not as fickle as a flame. She is an ocean. I knew from the first that I cannot own her, cannot tame her, but I am the only storm that moves her depths and stirs her tides. And that is more than enough.

I lower my lips to her neck and taste the alcohol and sandalwood of her perfume. I breathe slow and easy, feeling the lightness of love and the wordless unspooling of the sea of space that kept us apart. Impossible, it seems, that we were ever so distant. That there was ever a time where she existed and I was not with her. Everything that she is, every scent, taste, touch, makes me know I am home. She reaches up, dragging her slender fingers through my hair. "I missed you," I say.

"What's not to miss?" she asks, giving me a sly smile. I move to sit with her on the chaise, but she clucks her tongue. "You're not done yet. Keep rubbing, Imperator. Your Sovereign commands it."

"I think power's gone to your head." She glances up at me. "Yes, ma'am." I continue massaging her neck.

"I'm drunk," she mutters. "I can already feel the hangover."

"Thraxa's good at making it feel like a moral obligation to keep pace."

"Ten credits says we have to scrape Sevro off the patio tomorrow."

"Poor Goblin. All spirit, no body mass."

She laughs. "I put him and Victra in the west wing so we can actually get some sleep. Last time, I woke up in the middle of the night thinking a coyote was caught in the air recycler. I swear, at the pace they're going they'll be able to single-handedly populate Pluto in a few years."

She pats the cushion beside her. I join her on the chaise and wrap my arms around her. The lake breeze sighs through the trees. In the silence we share, I feel her heartbeat and wonder what her eyes see as they look out over the tops of the trees to the orange sky.

"Dancer was here," I say.

She makes a small noise of acknowledgment, to let me know she resents my reminder of the world beyond our balcony. "He's not happy with you."

"Half the Senate looked like they wanted to poison my wine."

"I warned you. Luna's changed since you were gone. The Vox Populi can't be ignored any longer."

"I noticed."

"Yet when they passed a resolution, you spat in their eye."

"And now they'll spit in mine."

"Seems that's the bed you made."

"Do they have the votes to block my request?"

"They might."

"Even if you apply pressure?"

"You mean even if I clean up your mess." It wasn't a question.

"I made the right decision," I say. "I know I did. You know I did.

They don't know war. They were afraid of being held responsible for failure. What was I supposed to do? Comb my hair while they protected their reputations?"

"Maybe you should learn from them."

"I'm not going to hold a poll in the middle of a war. You could have vetoed them."

"I could have. But then they'd cry that I was protecting my husband, and the Vox would gain even more supporters."

"Copper and Obsidian are still in play?"

"No. Caraval says the Coppers will back you. As goes Sefi, so goes Obsidian. What will she choose? You'd know better than I."

"I don't know," I admit. "She was against the Rain, but she came with me."

She's silent at that.

"You think I've shot us in the foot, don't you?"

"Does Dancer have anything else he can use against you?"

"No," I say. I know she doesn't believe me. And she knows I know, but she can't ask any more. Though I want to tell her about the emissaries, it would incriminate her as well. Sevro and I agreed it was a secret that must stay within the Howlers. She would be bound by oath to tell the Senate. And she tried so hard to honor her new oaths.

"Dancer's not the only one angry with me," I say. "Pax would hardly look at me at dinner."

"I saw."

"I don't know what to do."

"I think you do." She goes quiet. "We're missing this," she says eventually. "Life. The dinner tonight, I'll remember forever. The lightning bugs. The children in the yard. The smell of rain on its way." She looks over at me. "Just seeing you laughing. I shouldn't remember it. It should be one of thousands."

"What are you saying?"

"I'm saying that when my term of office ends in two years, maybe I won't run again. Maybe I let the torch pass to someone else. You hand the reins to Orion or Harnassus. Maybe the rest of this isn't our responsibility." A tiny, hopeful smile crosses her lips. "We will go back to Mars and live in my estate. We'll raise our children with your brother and sister's and put our lives into helping our family, our planet. And each night we'd have a dinner like this one. Friends could come and go in our house whenever they passed through. The door would always be open. . . ."

And an army would always have to guard it.

Her words carry away into the night, into the arms of the swaying trees, along with the current of the wind, up and up into the sky, where it seems all fantasies go. But I sit cold as a stone beside her, because I know she doesn't believe any of this. We've played the game far too long to walk away. I take her hand. And as my wife is quiet and the fantasy drifts away, our familiar friend, dread, creeps onto the balcony with us, because deep inside, in the shadowy chasms of ourselves, we know Lorn was right. For those who dine with war and empire, the bill always comes at the end.

And almost as if the world was listening to my thoughts, a knock comes at the door. Mustang answers it, and when she returns her face belongs to the Sovereign, not my wife. "It was Daxo. Dancer's called an emergency session of the Senate. They've moved your hearing up to tomorrow night."

"What does that mean?"

"Nothing good."

4

LYRIA

Welcome to the Worlds

Sky.

That's what my da would call the roof of stone and metal that stretched over our home in the mine of Lagalos. It's what we all used to call it, going back generations of our clan to the first Pioneers. *The sky be crumbling. The sky needs reinforcing.*

It stretched over us like a great shield, keeping us safe from the fabled Martian storms raging outside. There were dances for the sky, songs wishing it luck and blessings. I even knew two lasses named for it.

But the sky wasn't a shield. It was a lid. A cage.

I was sixteen years of knobby knees and freckles when I first saw the true sky. Took six years from the death of the Sovereign on Luna for the Rising to push the last of the Golds off our continent of Cimmeria. Two more years for them to finally free our mine from the Gray warlord who set up his own little kingdom in their absence.

Then the Rising came to Lagalos.

Our saviors looked more like manic Laureltide jesters than soldiers draped with trophies of gray and blond hair and iron pyramid badges. SlingBlades and spiked red helmets were painted on their chests. And standing at their front was a weary, bearded Red man old enough to be a grandfather. He had a large gun in one hand and in the other a tattered white flag with the fourteen-pointed morning star. He wept when he saw the bloated bellies and skeletal evidence of our starvation under the Gray warlord. His gun dropped to the floor, and though he was a stranger to us, he came forward and hugged me. "Sister," he said. Then he hugged the man beside me. "Brother."

Four weeks later, kind-faced men and women wearing white helmets and fourteen-pointed stars on their chests took us to the surface. I'll never forget their eyes. They were Yellow and Brown and Pink. They had bottles of water, sparkling sweet drinks and candy for the children. And they gave us clunky goggles marked with winged feet to cover our cave eyes from the sun. I didn't want to wear the goggles. Rather look at the true sky and its sun with my own eyes. But a kind Yellow nurse told me I might lose my sight. So on they went.

When the doors of the lift opened, we walked from a basin littered with ships, up metal stairs and out onto an endless plain of tall grass vibrating with the sound of insects, and I saw it: blue and vast, so large I felt I was falling up into it. The true sky. And there, hanging like a sullen coal on the impossible horizon, was the sun. Giving us warmth. Filling my eyes with tears. So small I could block it with a thumb. Our sun. *My* sun.

The Republic's relief ships arrived the next morning to bawdy choruses hurled out from the throats of young gallants and lasses. The ships were cleaner than anything I'd ever seen. White as my nephew's baby teeth as they coasted down. On their bellies blazed the star of the Republic. To us, then, the star meant hope.

"Reaper's compliments," a young soldier said as he handed me a chocolate bar. "Welcome to the worlds, lass."

Welcome to the worlds.

On the shuttle away from our mine, a video appeared before each of us, the hologram so lifelike I thought my fingers would touch the Gold face that sprung into the air. I'd seen her before, but here above ground on one of her ships, she seemed like a goddess from one of our songs. Virginia the Lionheart. Her eyes a terrifying gold. Her hair like spun silk held back from her poreless face. She shone brighter than that little coal of a sun. Making me feel little more than a shadow of a girl.

"Child of Mars, welcome to the worlds . . ." the young Sovereign began gently. "You are about to embark upon a great journey to your rightful place upon the surface of the planet your ancestors built. Your sweat, your blood, and that of your kin, gave this planet life. Now it is your turn to share in the bounty of mankind, to live and prosper in this new Solar Republic and pave a way for the next generation. My heart is with you. The hopes and dreams of people everywhere rise with you. Good luck and may you and yours find joy under the stars."

That was two years and a thousand broken promises ago.

Now, under a boiling sun, I hunch over the scant, piddling river beyond Assimilation Camp 121. My back bent and fingers crooked as I rub an abrasive brush into a pair of pants soiled by Ava's work in the slaughter yards where she kills cattle to fill our pot.

My arms, once ashen brown like most from Lagalos, are wiry and now baked dark by the sun and bitten ragged by the bugs that rise up out of the riverbed mud. The summers of the Cimmerian Plains are humid and thick with mosquitoes. I swat three away that've found a gap in the lyder flower paste.

I'm eighteen now with stubborn baby fat in my cheeks. My hair leaps from my head at a thick tangle. Like a rabid animal trying to escape my skull. I don't blame it. Eyes never rest long on me. The boys on Da's drillteam used to call me Mudbug for the color of my eyes. Da always said Ava's got the looks in our family. I've just got the temper.

Along the riverbank are hardpacked men and women—two score Gammas of my clan humming "The Ballad of Bloody Mary the Fool." My mother used to hum it as she worked. Rust-red hair bursts from under broad-brimmed hats and headwraps of bright cloth. Off the bank, fishermen laze on boats smoking tobacco as they drag their nets farther into the river.

Lambda doesn't let us use the Solar Republic washers in the center of the camp anymore. Bastards think they have the right, since they are the same clan as the Reaper. Never mind that they're as related to him as I am to bats that come out of the jungle at night to hunt for the camp's mosquitoes.

The Solar Republic ships don't come much anymore without a full military escort, what with the Red Hand marauders running mad in the South. Those that do come drop the supplies in little parachute crates from the sky. And the soldiers who actually land in the camp now cradle weapons instead of candy.

We see it on the HC news every day. Red Hand raids on helpless camps. Sons kidnapped, fathers killed, and the rest savaged. They claim they're bringing justice to my clan, the Gammas, for being the pets of our former oppressors. In every camp they raid, they purge us like a strain of diseased rats.

Ava believes the Republic will stop the Hand. That the Reaper will come with his howling legions and smite the bastards right and good. Or somesuch. She's always been a pretty fool. The Sovereign brought us out of the dirt and forgot us in the mud. The Reaper hasn't even been to Mars in years. Got more to worry about than his own Color, it seems.

Bitten ragged by the mosquitoes, I haul the basket up onto my head and make my way back to the camp. The pawing electricity of a coming storm fills the air. In the distance, across the green-stained savannah, huge thunderheads begin to bruise the sky purple and black. They're forming fast.

Heaps of trash hump the violent green landscape closer to the camp. Here and there range slim burner boys blackened dark with soot. They wear rags tied over their faces as they douse heaps of clothing and trash infected by the malaria outbreak with engine oil. The blazes choke the sky with cancerous black veins.

My brother, Tiran, is out there amidst the stacks, face wrapped like the rest, squinting into a blaze for one token an hour. In the mine, all he wanted to be was a Helldiver. It's all any of us wanted to be. I used to sneak downstairs late at night and don my father's workboots and his helmet and sit at the dinner table with forks and spoons pinched between my fingers, acting as if I were running a clawDrill.

But then my da fell into a pitviper nest and lost his legs. Soon after,

Mum died and the rest of Da went with her. I used to think my world permanent. That clansmen and women would always tip their heads to my father, that my mother would always be there to wake me and give me a spot of syrup before school. But that life is gone. More miners are lured up every day by the promise of freedom. And in their wake, the mines are bought by big companies from big cities and manned by robots stamped with a silver heel. Just like ours was. They say we're to receive a share soon as it makes a profit. We've yet to see so much as a half-credit chit.

A throaty din rises from Assimilation Camp 121 as I enter its open gates. It's a muck-soaked town of plastic, tin, and dog shit. Fifty thousand of us now in a place meant for twenty, with more coming every day. Gloomy squadrons of mosquitoes buzz low over the soup of the streets, searching for meat to suck. All the lads old enough for the Free Legions have gone to war. And those boys and girls who stay behind work shit jobs for food tokens so the old don't starve. No child dreams of being a Helldiver anymore, because in this new world there are no Helldivers left.

5

LYRIA

Camp 121

I MAKE IT TO MY FAMILY'S hut using the sheeting and wood planks that serve as roads through the mud. I slip under the mosquito netting just as thunder cracks open the sky overhead. Rain pours down, hammering the thin plastic roofs all down the narrow lane. Inside the dry hut, I'm greeted with the thick smell of stew. I set the basket down inside the door. Our home is five meters by seven, made of neoPlast stamped with the star of the Republic and a tiny little winged heel where the plastic meets the ground. It's separated into two small rooms by opaque plastic dividers that fall from the ceiling. The kitchen and living room in the front. The bunks in the back. My sister Ava is hunched over a little solar stove stirring a pot. She glances back at me as I stand panting.

"Either you're getting faster or the clouds are getting slower."

"Bit of both, I'd say." I rub the stitch in my side and sit down at the little plastic dinner table. "Tiran still burnin'?"

"That he is."

"Poor lad's gonna get drenched. Bloodydamn, it smells kind in here." I inhale the scent of stew.

Ava glows. "A bit of garlic found its way into the pot."

"Garlic? How'd that sneak through Lambda? They stop hoarding the new freight?"

"No." She goes back to stirring the pot. "One of the soldiers gave it to me."

"Gave? Out of the goodness of his high heart?"

"And that's not all." She hikes up her skirt to show off two brilliant blue shoes. Not government-issue clogs. Real shoes of leather and quality rubber.

"Bloodydamn. What you give him in return?" I ask in shock.

"Nothing!" Ava scrunches her nose at the accusation.

"Men don't give gifts for *nothing*."

"I'm married." She crosses her arms.

"Sorry. Forgot," I say with bite. Her husband, Varon, is as good a man as I've ever met, and as absent a one. He, along with our two eldest brothers, Aengus and Dagan, volunteered for the Free Legions right after we entered the camp. Last we heard from them was from a Legion com bank on Phobos. Three of them crowded together to fit into the frame. Said they were sailing with the White Fleet toward Mercury. Seems just yesterday I was following Aengus through the vents of Lagalos to look for fungus to fill his still.

"Where're the boys?" I ask.

"Liam's at the infirmary."

"Again?" A pang of pity goes through me.

"Another ear infection," she says. "Could you go visit him in the morning? You know how much—"

"Course," I interrupt. Liam, her second youngest, is just past six and has been blind from birth. He's always been my favorite. Sweet little thing. "I'll bring him some leftover candy if the other rats don't gobble it up."

"You spoil him."

"Some lads oughta be spoiled."

I find my niece, Ella, bundled up in her carriage by the table. She's playing with a little mobile of one of her brother's broken toys suspended above her. "How's my little haemanthus blossom on this *dreadful* stormy eve?" I say, poking her nose. She giggles and grabs my finger, then tries to eat it. "She got a mouth on her."

"I'll feed her after dinner. You mind checkin' Da's diaper?"

My father sits in his chair watching the HC box I stole from a Lambda too drunk to mind his tent. His eyes are pearly and distant, reflecting the static of the dead channel that writhes on the screen.

"Lemme help you with that, Da," I say. I change the channel till an image of a gravBike shooting over a Mercurian desert appears. Bad men pursue the roguish Blue hero, who looks not just a bit like Colloway xe Char.

"Is this all right?" I ask. Thunder rolls outside.

He doesn't answer. Doesn't even look at me, so I bite back the resentment and try to remember him as the man who used to take us to the deep mines. His rough hands would light the gas fire, and he'd whisper ghost stories of Golback the Dark Creeper or Old Shufflefoot in his hoarse voice. The flames from the fire would saw the air and he would boom out a hilarious laugh at our terrified faces.

I don't recognize this man . . . this creature wearing my father's skin. It just eats and shits and sits there watching the HC. Still, I shove the anger away, feeling guilty for it, and kiss him on the forehead. I tuck his blanket a little bit under his bearded chin and thank the Vale there's no soil in his diaper.

There's a clatter from the door as my sister's young sons bowl into the house, drenched in mud and rain. Next comes our remaining brother, Tiran, smelling of smoke from the burning stacks. He's the tallest in the family, but frighteningly thin. Most nights, he looks like a curled weed, hunched over the little books he writes for the children. Fills them with stories of castles and vales and flying knights. He whips his wet hair at us and tries to give Ava a hug. My sister shows off her shoes to her jealous boys with false modesty. They debate what one of the brighter blue colors on the tongues ought to be called while I set the dishes.

"Cerulean!" they decide. "Like Colloway xe Char's tattoos."

"Colloway xe Char. Colloway xe Char," Tiran mocks.

"Warlock's the best pilot in the worlds," Conn says in indignation.

Tiran scoffs. "I'd take the Reaper in a starShell against Char in a ripWing any day."

Conn puts his arms on his hips. "You're stupid. Warlock would blast him to bloody bits."

"Well, they're friends, so they won't be blasting each other to anything," my sister says. "They're too busy protecting your father and uncles, aren't they?"

"Do you think Da has met them?" Conn asks. "Char and the Reaper?"

"And Ares?" Barlow adds. "Or Wulfgar the Whitetooth?" He slams his hands like he's a menacing Obsidian. "Or Dancer of Faran! Or Thraxa au—"

"Aye, they're probably the best of friends. Now eat."

We eat dinner huddled around the plastic table as the rain drums the roof. There's barely enough room for bowls and elbows, but we layer around the thin soup and chatter on about the merits of ripWings against starShells in atmosphere. My sister smiles when the boys say the soup tastes better today.

After dinner, we gather around with Da to watch one of his programs. I break half of a Cosmos chocolate bar into seven pieces to share. I pocket my piece for Liam and smile when I see Tiran give his piece to Ava. No wonder he's so skinny. The program is a news show. The host a Violet who reminds me a bit of the helions—a tropical bird that lives off our trash. He has an incredible shock of white hair and a jaw you could carve granite with, but pathetically delicate hands for a man.

The very important man is reporting on the Reaper's Triumph in Hyperion City. My nephews all nudge each other as he theorizes that the next push will be toward Venus to finish off the Ash Lord and his daughter, the Last Fury, once and for all. My sister watches in silence, stroking her new shoes. So far our brothers and her husband have not been named in the casualty report that scrolls along the bottom of the holo.

Tiran leans toward the far-off world. He's always been the softest of our family, and the most eager to prove himself. Soon it'll be his turn. He becomes sixteen in just a few months. Then he'll leave all this mud behind for the stars. I can't help but resent him already. None of them should have left their family.

The boys don't see my sister's quiet desperation. The images of the HC dance in their Red eyes. The color. The spectacle of the Triumph on Luna. The glory of the greatest son of Red standing with his Gold wife—the Sovereign who promised us so much—lifting his clenched fist into the air as they howl. They think they could rise like the Reaper. They're too young to see our life is the lie behind the lights.

"Reaper! Reaper!" the crowd shouts.

My little nephews join in the chant. And I reach for my sister's hand, glaring at the HC, remembering the promises undelivered, and wonder if I'm the only one who misses the mines.

I wake in the night to a distant roar. The room is still. Sweat slicks my legs. I sit up in bed, listening. There's a clamor in the distance. The snoring of far-off engines. Mosquitoes buzz outside the netting that's wrapped around our bunks. "Aunt Lyria," Conn whispers from beside me. "What's that noise?"

"Quiet, love." I strain to hear. The engines fade. I push my legs off the edge of my bunk. Father's soft breathing comes from below. He's still asleep. My sister's bunk is empty. So is Tiran's sleeping pallet on the ground.

I slip past the mosquito netting and out of my bed in shorts and a cotton shirt soggy from the humidity. "Where are you going?" Conn asks. "Aunt Lyria . . ." I seal the netting behind me with the adhesive strip.

"Just going to take a peek, love," I say. "Go back to sleep." I slip on my sandals and leave the room. My sister is already awake, standing near the door and watching nervously as Tiran puts on his boots. "What's what?" I ask quietly. "Thought I heard a ship."

"Probably just some idiot SR airhead buzzing the camp," Tiran says.

"Not bloody likely," I snap. "We ain't had a supply ship land in a month."

"Lower your voice," he hisses. "The little ones'll hear."

"Well, if you weren't being thick, I wouldn't have to shout."

"Stop it, you two." Ava looks nervous. "What if it's the Red Hand?"

Tiran brushes his tangled hair from his eyes. "Don't get your frysuit in a twist. The Hand's hundreds of klicks south. Republic wouldn't let anyone in our airspace."

"Like that means pissall," I mutter.

"They own the skies," he replies like he's a Praetor.

"They don't even own their own cities," I say, remembering the bombings in Agea.

He sighs. "I'll go take a look. You both mind the house."

"Mind the house?" I laugh. "Stop acting the maggot. I'm coming with."

"No, you're not," Tiran replies.

"I'm just as fast as you."

"Not the bloody point. I'm the man of the house," he says, and I snort. "Remember what happened to Vanna, Torron's daughter? Girls shouldn't wander the township at night. Especially not us." He means Gamma, and he's right. I knew Vanna since I was a child. She was tattered flesh when they found her, hands cut off. We buried her by the treeline of the jungle south of the camp. "Besides, if I'm wrong, you gotta be here to help Ava and the little ones. I'll go take a look and I'll be back fastlike. I promise." He leaves without another word. Ava closes the door behind him. She wrings her hands and sits at the kitchen table. I sit down with her, picking at the scratches on the plastic top in irritation. *Man of the house.*

"Slag this." I stand up. "I'm gonna go have a look."

"Tiran's already gone!"

"Please. His balls have barely dropped. I'll be back in a tick." I head to the door.

"Lyria . . ."

"What?"

She grabs our lone frying pan from the kitchen. "At least take this."

"In case I find eggs? Fine. Fine." I take the pan. "Might want to get water and food ready just in case." She nods and I leave her behind.

The night is grim and humid as air in a smoker's mouth. By the time I've made it out of Gamma township and into the main camp, a tongue of sweat licks down the small of my back. It's quiet but for the hissing insects. A withered gaboon lizard watches me from the roof of a refugee domicile as it chews on a night moth. Lights glow from the far end of the camp where the landing pads lie. Eyes glint out from plastic doorways as I pass, peering out from behind mosquito netting. The streets are empty. I'm afraid in a way I never was in the mines. Feeling smaller now than I did in our hut.

There's men's voices arguing ahead. I creep carefully forward till I'm crouched behind a stack of discarded cargo containers. Two rusty pelican transport vessels have landed on the concrete pads. One is painted with the face of a lithe Pink model drinking a bottle of Ambrosia, a sweet pepper cola beverage that's given half the camp cavities. She smiles and winks at me, her mouth full of white, gleaming teeth. The lights of the ships blaze in the predawn, silhouetting the group of men from our camp who've woken and gone out to inspect the landed ships. My brother is amongst them, loitering in the back self-consciously. I suddenly feel guilt for snorting when he said "man of the house." He's just a boy. My boy, my little brother trying to be big. The clansmen are exchanging words with another group of men who've come down the ships' ramps. These ones are Reds too, but they carry weapons and long bandoliers stocked with ammunition across their bare chests.

The new men are asking where to find the Gammas. There's an argument amongst the men from our camp, then one of them is pointing toward our township. Another shoves him, but soon several other men begin to point not just at our homes, but toward Tiran and several others amongst their group. The other men drift away from my brother and the three other Gammas. The smallest of the men from the ship says something, but I don't catch it. One of the Gammas rushes him just as the man lifts a long dark object from his side. Acid-green light churns in the ammunition globe of his plasma rifle, then lunges from the muzzle in a rippling ball that gashes the darkness. It cleaves clean through the center of the man. He teeters to the ground like a township drunk. I'm frozen to the spot. My brother flees with the other pair of Gammas. One of the outsiders raises his rifle.

Metal chatters like a broken silk-threading machine.

My brother's chest erupts. The other gunmen shatter the quiet night, flashing and bleeding fire from their weapons. Tiran spasms, jerks. Not falling quickly. But stumbling one step, two steps, then another gunshot cracks the air and he is tumbling. Half his head is gone. A wailing cry rises from my belly. The whole world rushes past and goes silent as I stare at that shadowy mound in the mud.

Tiran . . .

The first man to fire walks over to my brother's body and rakes the corpse with the plasma weapon. Then he looks up at me, the acid-green fire illuminating a face like a demon's. It's not a man. It's a Red woman with terrible scars covering half of her face.

"Justice to Gamma!" Synced to the speakers on both of the ships behind her, her voice bellows out into the night. "Death to the collaborators! Justice to Gamma!"

6

EPHRAIM

Eternal City

I YAWN IN THE HUMID DARK, craving a burner because the vapor inhaler I'm sucking on is about as satisfying as fucking through a tarpaulin sheet. My left foot is numb and sweating through the sock in its rubber shoe, and my right arm is bent so awkwardly into the stone that my knock-off Valenti chronometer is drilling into the bone of my wrist with every. Arterial. Pulse.

The only thing that has kept me sane over the past nine hours has been the holocontacts I bought off the rack from that lemur-looking bastard, Kobachi, on 198th, 56th, and 17th in Old Town. But the contacts shorted out, and now I've got a corneal abrasion and worse, plenty of time to kill. Perfect.

I try in vain to stretch. The stone box doesn't give me much room to wriggle my 1.75-meter frame. My main grudge against ancient Egyptians isn't that they pioneered the institution of mass slavery for public works, it's that they were all so damn tiny. Still smells like the old raisin we dragged out of it late last night before the delivery.

I check my watch. It was a gift from my late fiancé. One of the cheap silvery types cobbled together by half-blind immigrant low-Colors in sweatshops deep in the armpits of Luna. Probably Tycho

City. Maybe Endymion or the Mass. Somewhere half a world away from the beating heart of Hyperion—where I am currently entombed. He didn't know it was a knockoff, so he paid nearly sixty percent market value, half his quarterly pay. His face glowed when he gave it to me. I didn't have the heart to tell him he could have bought it for the price of a decent bottle of vodka. Poor kid.

Check the watch again. Almost time.

Two minutes to midnight, only several hours left of dusk before Hyperion is plunged into the last dark month of summer. Dark or light, a day in Hyperion never truly ends. The caretakers of the day just lock their doors and hand the reins of the town over to the nocturnal creatures. Under Gold it wasn't exactly a Pink's paradise. But now, it's the law of the jungle when the lights go out. Outside the museum, the hot city will be stretching and crooning in the sweaty dusk, readying to make some trouble. On the lamplit Promenade, decent citizens will skitter to their private housing complexes, fleeing the yapping of young music and the roar of hoverbike gangs echoing up from Lost City.

Hyperion. Jewel of Luna. The Eternal City. She's a beautiful wartime mess. So much to look at, you can only afford to see what you want to see. If you plan on staying sane, that is.

But here, in the Hyperion Museum of Antiquities, behind thick walls of marble is a world with a different set of rules. During day hours, packs of drooling lowColor schoolchildren and Martian and Terran immigrants waddle their way through the marble corridors, rubbing snotty noses against glass containment boxes. At night, though, the museum is a fortress crypt. Impenetrable from the outside, occupied only by a contingent of pale night guards and the dead residents of crypts, statues, and paintings. The only way in was to become a resident. So we bribed a docker and snuck aboard a freighter from Earth as it landed at Atlas Interplanetary. A freighter that happened to hold numerous relics liberated from the private stash of some exiled Gold overlord dead or fled to Venus. Probably old Scorpio. Whole slew of goodies. Fourteen paintings from neoclassical Europe, a crate of Phoenician urns, twenty-five crates of Roman scrolls, and four sarcophagi.

What was yesterday filled with mummified Egyptians is tonight filled with freelancers.

By now the janitorial technicians will be herding up their robot charges and moving to the east wing. A team of security guards occupies a headquarters in the basement.

Tick. Tock. Tick. Tock.

I'm sick of waiting. Sick of the carousel of thoughts in my brain. I stare at the watch, willing the hands forward on their cheap gears that lose seconds every day. Can't think of anything but a ghost and how each tick, each tock, takes me farther from him. Farther from the ridiculous slicked-back hair he wore because he thought it made him look like a holostar I liked, or the knockoff Duverchi jackets he'd wear thinking it hid the farmboy underneath. That was his problem—always trying to be something he wasn't. Always trying to be *more*. Ate him up in the end and spat him out.

I pull my zoladone dispenser from my pack. I thumb the silver cylinder and it dispenses a black pill the size of a rat's pupil into my hand. Particularly wicked new designer drug. Absurdly illegal. Jacks up your dopamine and suppresses activity in the bit of gray matter responsible for empathy. Spec ops teams ate Zs like candy during the Battle of Luna. If you have to melt a city block, it's better to save the tears till you're back in your bunk.

I keep the dose low. One milligram worth of emotion-numbing molecules lances through my blood. The thoughts of my fiancé lose their dimensionality, becoming nothing but flat, monochrome pictures in a faded memory.

Tick. Tock. Tick. Tock.

Beep.

Shine time. I click my com once. Three more clicks echo.

Then there's a grating sound from the stone. It begins to move on its own. Blue light from the warehouse overheads seeps through the cracks as the lid of the sarcophagus levitates. A dark mass stands above me, holding the stone lid in the air as if it were made of neo-Plast.

"Evening, Volga," I mouth in gratitude to the giant woman. I sit up and feel a series of satisfying pops as my spinal cord stretches. Half my age, my Obsidian accomplice smiles with a mouth mangled by second-rate dental work. Unlike ice Obsidians, her face is absent the dense wind calluses that usually hide the sloping of cheekbones. Volga's small for an Obsidian, lean and a stunted six and a half feet. It makes her look less threatening than the average crow. It's not what her makers intended. She was born in a lab, courtesy of a Society breeding program. Poor kid didn't measure up with the rest of the crop and was tossed down to Earth for slave labor.

Met her five years back at a loading dock outside Echo City. I had delivered an item to a collector and had to celebrate with a few cocktails. Volga found me ten drinks and two centimeters deep in a pool of my own blood in an alley, mugged, cut, and left for dead by two local blackteeth. She carried me to a hospital and I paid her back with a ride to Luna, the one place she really wanted to go. Been following me around ever since. Teaching her the trade is my own little pet project.

Like me, she wears a black neoPlast suit to hide her thermal signature. She's still holding the lid of the sarcophagus above my head in the gloom of the museum's warehouse.

"You can stop showing off now," I mutter.

"Do not be jealous, tiny man, that I can lift what you cannot lift."

"Shhh. Don't bark so damn loud."

She winces. "Sorry. I thought Cyra turned off the security system."

"Just shut up," I say irritably. "Don't skip in a minefield." The old legion adage makes me feel even older than does the old ache in my right knee.

"Yes, boss." She makes an embarrassed face and sets the stone down gently before extending a hand to lift me out. I groan. Even with the Z, I feel every drink and snort and puff of my forty-six years. I blame the legion for stealing a good quarter of them. The Rising for stealing three more before I wised up and split. And then myself for spending all the rest like there'd be more coming at the end of the rainbow.

I don't need a mirror to tell me I'm the secondhand model of myself. I've got the telltale swollen face of a man who's gone one too many rounds with the bottle, and a slight body even a decade in legion gravity gymnasiums couldn't broaden.

I gather the green wrappers from my dinner of sirloin cubes and Venusian ginger seaweed and spray an aerosol can of blackmarket DNA into the sarcophagus before stuffing the can and the garbage into my backpack. Up goes my bodysuit's facial hood and I motion to Volga to don hers. We find the other two members of my team past a stack of crates four meters high, crouched in front of the security door leading out of the warehouse.

"Top of the evening," my team's cat, Dano, a young, pimply Red, says without looking back. "Could hear your knees creaking from a hundred meters, Tinman. Need some street grease in them. I know a louse at a chop shop who'll do you good."

I ignore him and his Terran overfamiliarity.

I need more Lunese associates. Hell, I'd even take a grumpy Martian. Terrans are all such talkers.

My Green locksmith, Cyra, another Terran, is on a knee working the interior of the biometric lock. Her gear is set out on the floor near the door, where she'll run support. Bit twitchy, that one. She doesn't usually like coming to the dancefloor. I've hired Cyra sporadically over the past few years, but we're not close. She's like most Limies—petulant and selfish, with a processor in place of a heart. Especially nasty to Volga. Doesn't bother me. I came to the conclusion at the age of nine that most people are liars, bastards, or just plain stupid. She's a good hacker, and that's all I care about. There's few enough of them freelancing these days. Corporations, criminal and reputable alike, are gobbling up all the talent.

Both Cyra and Dano are short, and the only way to tell them apart in their hooded black bodysuits is the sizable paunch around Cyra's midsection, that and the fact that Dano is doing the splits stretching for his part in the play, and humming an asinine Red ditty to himself.

I mind Dano less than Cyra. I've known him since he was a street rat fresh off the boat from Earth, pickpocketing on the Promenade with more acne on his face than hair in his head.

Cyra's hands work the innards of the door, her left holding an output jack that transmits a wireless signal from the door to the hardware in her head. Two metal crescents packed with hardware and two hardline uplinks embedded in her skull run from her temples, over her ears, and back toward the base of her cranium. I see their bulge from underneath her thermal hood.

"Door alarm?" I ask, when she leans back from the door.

"Off, obviously," she snaps, voice muffled through the hood. "The magnetic seal is dead." She glances over at Volga, who has kneeled to unfold her compact assault rifle from its black case. "Planning to break your rule tonight, crow?"

"Wait, are we murder positive?" Dano asks eagerly.

"No. We're not breaking any rules," I reply. "But if chance strikes, the pale lady is my walking, talking insurance policy. You know what they say. Hell hath no fury like a woman packing a railgun." Volga's gloved hands assemble the black weapon. She pulls free three curved clips of ammunition and attaches them to the outside of her suit with bonding tape. Each clip is marked with a colored band coordinating with the type of projectile—venom paralytic, electrical disrupter, hallucinogenic round. Never killing rounds. Damn inconvenient having a killing-machine bodyguard who refuses to kill.

I've no such reservations. I touch the pistol on my own hip, making sure the leg holster is tight. Muscle reflex by this point. I look back at Cyra. "You going to make me ask about the rest of the alarms?"

"Limey couldn't get all of 'em," Dano says from the ground where he contorts his leg behind his head in a bizarre hamstring stretch.

"That right?"

"Yeah," Cyra mutters.

Dano looks over at me, his face hidden behind the tight black plastic of his thermal. "Told you we shoulda hired Geratrix."

"Geratrix is Syndicate now," I mutter.

Dano bows his head in mock sorrow. "Another one for the bloody black."

"It's not my fault," Cyra says in a low voice. "They updated their system. New protocols are government. Would take me near thirty minutes to punch in. Shit, it'd take a team of Republic astral hackers at least twelve—"

I hold up a hand. "Hear that?" I whisper. They listen. "That's the sound of your take getting cut in half."

"Half?"

"Half a job, half pay."

Cyra's got a temper on her as short as a tick's tooth. Her hand drops to the multigun on her hip. Still, Volga takes one step toward her and Cyra looks like a kitten hearing thunder. I bend on a knee in front of the Green. "It's not my fault . . ." she says. I take her chin through the mask and guide it so she's looking at me.

"Calm down, and tell me the problem." I snap my fingers. "Today, pissant."

"I can't access the Conquerors Exhibit systems," she admits.

"At all?"

"It's on an isolated server. Real relics in there, real security."

I feel a spasm of annoyance in my left eyelid. Damn. Dano's gonna have to do some acrobatics. "You know how I hate surprises, Cyra. . . ."

"Told you we shoulda bought the gravBelts," Dano says.

"Say 'I told you we shoulda' one more time. See what happens." He meets my eyes, then glances down at the floor. Thought so. "Spider gloves are good enough," I say. "Recyclers on." Dano, Volga, and I pull our recyclers from our bags and strap them over our thermals' mouth holes. "I trust you still have the doors figured. . . ."

She nods.

"Thirty seconds in each room," I remind them as Volga slings her gun on her back and approaches the door. Dano rolls up from his stretch and Volga pushes a large flat magnet against the door. It makes a dull thump as it locks onto the metal. We stare at the magnet as its sound reverberates. Through the door our voices won't be heard, but that might have been. I look to Cyra. She shakes her head. Decibel levels were too low. Clear, Volga wraps her massive mitts around the handle.

My body welcomes the adrenaline, sucking it down like water on cracked asphalt. I look at the watch and feel nothing. My focus narrows to the here and now. I grin.

"No one better sprain their fucking ankle," I say, warming up my legs. "Go on, V. Shine time." Volga heaves on the door, rolling it back into the wall.

"And grid one is down," Cyra says quietly into our coms. Dano goes first into the hall on sound-dampening shoes. I go next and look to see if Volga's following. She's right behind me, freakishly silent despite her size. Cyra stays behind, monitoring the security systems and the guard level.

Down a narrow staff corridor lies another heavy security door. *"Hold,"* Cyra says. *"Grid two is down. Twenty-nine, twenty-eight . . ."* Volga puts a mechanical lever under the door and activates it. The heavy door slides upward, jolting along with the lever. We shimmy under the door. A painting of a furious warhorse strapped to a chariot is suspended mid-stride from the ceiling. In the chariot is an archer firing at men in bronze armor and horsehair helms. I stand quickly to look around the vast room. Weeping stone children peer down from the floral columns. Great frescoes explode with color along marble walls. Soon the floor pressure sensors, cameras, and lasers will come back on.

"Twenty."

A sense of nostalgia sweeps over me as we run across the floor. Seems just yesterday I was here as a legion pledge. I remember boarding the tram to come to the city center wearing the winged pyramid pin they give us, puffing my chest out when highColors would nod to me or lowColors would step out of my path. Stupid kid. He thought that pin made him a man. It just made him a pet. And nowadays it'll get you scalped.

"Eight. Seven . . ."

After three more halls and a stitch in my side later as I try to keep up with my younger crew, we reach the Conquerors Exhibit, where we prop open the door with the lever and shimmy under. Carefully, we stand on a narrow slip of metal, just shy of the marble floor that has the inbuilt pressure sensors.

The room is as domineering as its subjects. Built by enraptured

Golds to honor their psychotic ancestors who conquered Earth, it is grand and brutal, and unchanged by the Republic except for a few modifications. They've included a list of the conquered amongst the conquerors. Representations of pre-Color humans stand beside casualty statistics. One hundred and ten million died for Gold to rule. Then their bombers dropped solocene into the troposphere and neutered an entire race. Didn't even have to convert them to the Color hierarchy. Just had to wait a century for them to die out. Bloodless genocide. Give one thing to the Conquerors. They were efficient.

Pricks.

At the center of the exhibit, under a stone archway with the legend CONQUERORS EXHIBIT, twenty ancient Ionic columns line an ascending stairway. At the top, a Delphic temple sits, and inside that, past priceless relics encased in duroglass, lies the object of my collector's desire. It is a sword of the first overlord, a razor belonging to the great bastard, hero of the Conquerors, Silenius au Lune. The Lightbringer.

"That don't look so scary," Dano said when we first got the contract.

I smiled and nodded to Volga. "What if she were holding it?"

"She'd look scary waving a bloodydamn muffin."

"If I had a muffin, I would eat it," Volga said.

The blade sits behind two fingers of duroglass and is on loan to the museum from a private collector for only one week longer. Liberation Day is a perfect time for it to go missing. Volga and I scan the ceiling of the exhibit, looking for the telltale sign of a drone garage. We see it in the top left corner of the room, a small titanium flap built into the marble. I nod to Volga, and she slips on her spider gloves and jumps onto the wall. They stick to the marble and she crawls along the wall till she's hanging beneath the garage door. She pulls four laser nodes from her pack and puts them on either side of the door and activates them. Two green lasers crisscross over the door. She gives me an eager thumbs-up and looks for more garages.

I nudge Dano. He's up.

The boy does an ironic two-step dance on the narrow slip of the doorframe, jumps up onto the wall with his spider gloves, then pushes off with his legs, backflipping onto a glass case holding a Gold war helmet. He catches himself, turns, then leapfrogs case to case till he can jump onto one of the Ionic columns. He hits it midway up, hugs it and shimmies up. As he moves, I summon the autoflier from its garage five klicks away via my datapad. It drives autonomously through traffic toward the museum. Dano moves along the columns like some sort of human flea till he's picked his way directly above the glass case. He lets himself fall, turning in the air so he lands on all fours in a way that makes my knees ache just to watch.

Dano stands and delivers an obnoxious bow before pulling his laser cutter from his pack. The glass glows as he cuts a circular hole into it. Then, with a triumphant smile, he plucks up the blade and holds it aloft.

The alarm goes off on schedule.

A high-pitched frequency screams out of speakers. It would shred our eardrums if we didn't have sonic plugs. As it is, it's little more than the annoying whine of a hungry dog. A second security door closes behind us, sealing us in. Two nodes on the ceiling lower and begin to pump disabling gas into the room. Does nothing with our recyclers running. Up high on the wall, the drone garage opens and a metal drone rips out of its hiding place, right into Volga's laser grid. It smokes down to the floor in four pieces. A second follows and meets the same fate as she shoots out the cameras. At the windows, metal security doors fall to block us in. I stand still like a conductor at the center of his orchestra. All these variables falling into place just as I planned. And a deep, formless depression falls on me as the adrenaline fades.

"Locksmith, find your exit," I mutter into my com.

Volga drops from her place on the wall to join me. She moves excitably, still young enough to be impressed by this. Dano hops along the columns back to the arch, where he graffities profanity with his laser drill. "The razor?" I ask.

He twirls it in his hand. It's meant for a man twice his size. "A nasty little dick tickler."

"The razor," I say again.

"Course, boss." He flips it to me casually. I snag it out of the air. Its handle is too big for my hand. Real ivory exterior and inlaid with gold filigree. The rest is brutally economical. In whip form it coils like a thin, sleeping snake. Eager to be rid of it, I shove it in a foam carry case and tuck it into my pack.

"All right, kids." I open the canister of custom acid and tip it onto the marble floor. "Time to go."

7

EPHRAIM

The Arbiter

THE MORNING AFTER THE HEIST, on my least favorite day of the year, I drain the vodka from my glass, waiting for the arbiter to finish his inspection. "So, is there a verdict yet?" I ask without bothering to hide my impatience. The slender man makes a show of remaining silent at the desk over which he has been hunched for the better part of an hour. It's overdramatic White slush. Anemic assholes think it profound to feign an air of aloofness, hiding behind contracts and commerce the way spiders hide and wait behind their webs. Two hundred were sentenced to life in Deepgrave during the Hyperion Trials for their part in the Gold judicial system. Should have been ten thousand. Rest were saved by the Amnesty declared by the Sovereign.

Bored, I survey the rest of the penthouse. It is painfully tasteful, done up in the restrained ostentation popular in Luna's upper circles—minimalist decor with rose-quartz floors and large windows that look out over the glowing nightscape. On a moon where three billion souls clamor atop each other to breathe, only the offensively rich can afford to waste space.

It reminds me of so many of the decadent flats I encountered as a high-end claims investigator for Piraeus Insurance, before the Rising. Back when I was the help.

HighColors looked down on Grays because we took out the trash. LowColors hated us because they were the trash. Everyone else feared us, because for seven hundred years we have been the all-purpose knife of the state. Obsidians? Circus freaks, the lot of 'em. Grays do work. We are adaptable, efficient, and bred for systematic loyalty. Little has changed for most of them: new masters, same collar.

I yawn. I'm thinking too much again, so I pop a zoladone, stand and pace as the drug leads my wandering thoughts back to my employer with a cold, distant hand.

Oslo, if that is in fact his name, is an inoffensive, impossibly meticulous creature with a dreadful sense of calm that borderlines on the robotic. Slender, and professional in his white business tunic with a starched high collar and sleeves to his knuckles. His skin is squid ink black. His head bald and the irises of his eyes an unsettling white. He adjusts the digital monocle on his right eye.

"I do believe this is the item my clients requested," he says in a harmonic baritone.

"As I said. Can we wrap this up?" He leans closer to the blade one last time before straightening and sheathing it very carefully into a gel-insulated metal briefcase.

"Citizen Horn, as ever, you delivered the requested item in a timely manner." Oslo turns back to me, typing into his datapad. "You will note that the agreed-upon sum has been deposited into your Echo City account."

I pull up my own datapad to check. His right eyebrow goes up. "I trust everything is satisfactory."

"Yut," I mutter.

"Yut?" he says in curiosity. "Oh yes, legion speak. Denoting an affirmation, usually done to convey affirmative sarcasm to a disliked officer."

"It's called dog tongue," I say. "Not 'legion speak.' "

"Of course." He touches his chest. "In fact I studied it extensively. I suppose you could say I'm a bit of a military enthusiast. The traditions. The organization. 'Merrywater *ad portas*,' " he says with a smile, using the phrase that seven centuries of legionnaires have shouted in memory of John Merrywater, the American who almost turned the tide of the Conquering by invading Luna—a reminder that the enemy is always at the gate.

I let it go, reminded of something the Ash Lord said to my cohort as a valedictory speech. "Those you protect will not see you. They will not understand you. But you are the Gray wall between civilization and chaos. And they stand safe in the shadow you cast. Do not expect praise or love. Their ignorance is proof of the success of your sacrifice. For we who serve the state, duty must be its own reward."

Or something like that. Good branding. Works like a charm on sixteen-year-old gray matter.

"Now, what is next on your mysterious employer's list?" I ask. "The sword of Alexander? The Magna Carta? The blackened heart of Kuthul Amun? I know. The knickers of the Sovereign herself. If she wears any . . ."

"There will be nothing else."

"Between you and me, I doubt she wears—wait, what?"

"There will be nothing else, Citizen Horn," Oslo says, picking up the briefcase containing the razor.

"Nothing?"

"Correct. My client has found this business relationship most satisfactory, but this piece will be the final acquisition, completing their collection. Thusly will we conclude our affiliation. Your services will not be required in the future."

"Well, my bank account's sorry to see you go," I say, feeling a nasty hollowness knowing no job is waiting in the wings. It's the first time in three years I've not had one on deck. "But nothing good can last forever, eh?" I stand and offer my hand to the taller White. He shakes it gently, and I hold on. The platinum rings on my forefinger dig into his tissue-thin skin. "So you're still not even going to give me a hint about who I've been stealing for all this time?" He jerks his hand away and I narrow my eyes at him. "Just a hint."

Oslo stares at me intensely.

"Why did curiosity kill the cat?" he asks me.

"Is telling riddles part of the job requirement?"

He smiles. "Because the cat stumbled upon the anaconda."

I linger in the suite after Oslo has left, long enough to dull the bitterness of his words with a couple more glasses of vodka. Out the window, my city of towers writhes. She looks prettier in the dark.

Idly, I cycle through the contents of my address book, looking for a distraction. It's a sea of detritus: bodies I've explored, relationships I've stretched past fraying. And floating amidst that wretched digital sea, standing in front of the city that never sleeps, surrounded by a billion breathing mouths, I feel the dark creep of despair. I pour one last drink, willing the numbness to spread.

A half day later, after a nap and a sobering plate of Terran noodles, I meet my crew to disburse the funds, though I hardly feel like company, on account of the date. They're huddled in a booth in an uppity South Promenade bar on the fringe of Old Town, drinking vibrantly colored cocktails. Volga twirls a pink umbrella between massive fingers. The bar itself is located inside the gutted carcass of an old advertising dirigible that someone renovated in an attempt to commercialize irony. Seems to be working despite the wartime rationing. The place buzzes with soldiers, packs of slick, suited Silvers, new-monied Greens and Coppers. All the ones near the right levers to make cash when the free market opened, now surrounded by the gaggles that attend them like brightly plumed vultures. It's mostly midColors, and there's been more than a few nervous glances aimed at Volga. The big girl has ordered me something called a Venusian Fury. It's dark as its namesake, Atalantia au Grimmus, and tastes like licorice and salt. Something in it makes the back of my eyes buzz and my groin swell. "What do you think?" she asks hopefully.

"Tastes like the ass end of the Ash Lord." I push it away. She looks downcast at the table. In my haze, pity is slow to come, and dull when it does. I hate bars like this.

"You know what the Ash Lord's ass tastes like?" Cyra asks.

"Look how old he is," Dano says, taking a break from staring at a beautiful slip of a Pink at the bar, who looks nervously at his nasal piercings. His head is buzzed in popular fashion with Obsidian dragons. "Tinpot's been around long enough to try everything." I don't reply, trying to hold on to the buzz left over from Oslo's vodka. I'll need it where I'm going.

"Whose idea was this commercial shithole?" I ask.

"Not mine," Dano says, holding up his hands. "Not nearly enough bare tits in this place."

"It was mine," Cyra says defensively. "It was featured in *Hyperion Weekly*. You know, Eph, it *is* humanly possible to enjoy something different. Something new."

" 'New' generally means someone's just trying to make money off something old."

"Whatever. It's better than the black-hole dives you visit to pickle your liver. Least here I'm not worried about getting an infection just by walking in the door."

"Let's get this over with." I pull up my datapad so they can all see, and transfer the funds into each of their accounts. Sure, they'd see the balances change on their own pads if I'd just done it over the net. But there's something incredibly human and satisfying for them to see my thumb disburse the money. "All done," I say. "Six hundred apiece."

"Even for Limey?" Dano asks. "Thought she was getting half."

"What the hell does it matter to you?" Cyra snaps.

"The rest of us did our jobs without a bloody hitch." He goes back to looking at the Pink girl, who's talking with her friends. "No reason we shouldn't get a little bonus for that action."

"I need no bonus," Volga says.

Dano sighs. "You ain't helping the cause, love."

"What the shit is your damage?" Cyra glares at Dano past Volga between them. "Always jacking on about my business? Why don't you tend your own and focus on catching diseases from Pink slips."

I lurch to my feet. "All right, this was fun. Try not to catch anything."

"And he's out like a Drachenjäger." Dano checks his newest shiny chronometer. This one has rubies embedded in the hands. "Two minutes flat."

"When's the next job?" Cyra asks.

"Yeah, boss," Dano says. "When's the next job? Cyra's got bills to pay."

She flips him the crux and stares at me with more desperation than she probably means to show. It's pitiful. "So? Your man's got another job, right?"

"Not this time. We're all done."

"What do you mean?"

"What I said." Seeing rain slithering down the windows, I pop the collar of my jacket.

"Ephraim," Volga says plaintively. "You just arrived. Stay for a drink. We can order you something else?" She stares up at me with those big mopey eyes, and for a moment I consider it, until I hear a telltale hush of the patrons and turn to see two towering figures emerge from outside through the dirigible's metal door. Golds. They wear black jackets with legion epaulets, their shoulders eclipsing the heads of the other patrons. They blithely survey the room with entitled eyes, before one of them catches sight of Dano's Pink and strides to the bar. The others make room and he introduces himself without a care in the world. There's an iron griffin pin on his chest. Arcos spawn. Dano's eyes go down as the Gold's hand drifts to the Pink's waist.

"Boss . . ." Dano says, eyeing me warily.

I realize my hand has drifted to the butt of the pistol under my jacket.

Bloodydamn Aureate. We should have purged the lot of them, or exiled them to the Core. But that chance is gone. All for the war effort.

"Just one drink, Ephraim," Volga says plaintively. "It will be fun. We can tell each other stories. And share jokes, as friends do."

"It's always the same story!"

As I leave the dirigible in the gravLift, the warm laughter of one of the Gold youths chases me down into the night.

8

LYSANDER

The Gulf

The baking sand warms my feet. They're smaller than I remember. Paler. And the gulls that careen overhead much larger, much fiercer as they spin and dive into the water of a sea so blue I cannot tell where ocean ends and sky begins. Gentle waves call to me. I've been here before, but I cannot remember when or how I came to be on this beach.

A man and woman are in the distance, their feet leaving slender paths that the waves, in time, slowly devour, step by step, then all at once till they are gone as if they were never there. I call to them. They begin to turn, but I do not see their faces. I never do. Something is behind me, casting a shadow over them, over the sand, darkening the beach and the sea as the wind builds to a feral howl.

My body jerks awake.

I'm alone. Far from the beach, drenched in sweat upon my sleeping pallet. A ventilator whirs rhythmically in the dimness of my room and I shudder a breath. The fear fades. It was just a dream.

Above me on the bulkhead, the words of my fallen house glare down at me, etched into the metal. *LUX EX TENEBRIS*. "Light from darkness." And spinning outward from those words like the spokes of a wheel are the idealist poems of youth, the wrathful, slashing script of adolescence, when I was all blood and fury and ruled by wilder passions. Then, finally, the first fledgling steps of wisdom as I began to realize how terrifyingly small I really am.

My father never seemed small. I remember him and his immense calm. The smile lines around his eyes. His unruly hair, his slender hands, how they sat folded in his lap when he listened. There was a vast, settled peace inside him, a tranquility given to him by his father, Lorn au Arcos, who stressed duty and honor under the banner of the griffin. Lost things to this world. Though somewhere out there, the griffin still flies.

My memory is a formidable thing. In many ways it is my grandmother's great legacy, her teachings preserved in me. Despite that, my mother's face is a night shade in my mind, always roving in the chasms, slipping beyond my grasp. I've heard she was wild, a woman of vast ambition. But history is so often molded from tainted clay by those who remain. I know more of her from my grandmother's mouth than from my own memory. Such was my grandmother's grief after her passing that no servant was permitted to speak her name aloud. Who was she? The few pictures I've found on the holoNet are all obscured, taken from a distance. As if she were a figment even cameras could not capture. Now time erodes her face in my mind like waves did the footprints in the sand.

I was young when my parents' starship went down over the sea. They say it was terrorists. Outriders from the Rim.

Only when I read the few poems my mother left behind in her notebooks do I feel her heart beat against my spine. Her arms wrapped around my shoulders. Her breath in my hair. I sense that strange magic of her that my father so loved.

"The night terrors again?" The voice of my teacher startles me. He stands looking into my room, Golden eyes dark pools in the starship's night-cycle lighting. His powerful shoulders fill the doorway and he bends at the neck, wary of the low doorframe. The engines hum soothingly beyond my small metal room. The place had space enough when I was a boy. But twenty now, I feel like a potted plant spilling root and limb from a cracking clay bowl. Books fill the spaces between my bunk, tiny closet, and lavatory. Salvaged, stolen, purchased, and found over the last ten years. My new prize, a third edition of the *The Aeronaut,* sits by my bedside.

"Just a dream," I say, wary of showing vulnerability in his eyes because I know how young the Martian still thinks I am. I swing my slender legs from the bed and bind my mess of hair behind my head with a band. "Have we arrived?"

"Just."

"Verdict?"

"My goodman, do I look like your valet?"

"No. She was much fairer. With better bedside manner."

"Adorable, pretending you just had one."

I raise an eyebrow. "You should talk, prince of Mars."

Cassius au Bellona grunts. "So are you going to sleep the day away, or get up and see for yourself?" He nods for me to follow; I do, as I have for ten years. I smell whiskey in his wake.

Once, the worlds called Cassius the Morning Knight, protector of the Society, slayer of Ares. Then he murdered his Sovereign, my grandmother, and let the Rising tear down the very Society he swore to protect. He let Darrow destroy my world and bring chaos to the Society. I can never forgive him for that, but neither can I repay the debt I owe him. He kept Sevro au Barca from killing me. He pulled me from the ashes of Luna and the chaos that followed, and for ten years he has protected me, given me a home, a second family.

We could be mistaken for brothers and often are. Our hair has that same luster of gold, though his is curled and mine straight. My eyes are pale as yellow crystal. His are dark gold. He's half a head taller than I, and broader in the shoulders and manlier in the features—a thick, pointed beard, a prominent bold nose, where my face is thin and patrician, like most from the Palatine Hill. I wish I did not look so delicate.

My name is Lysander au Lune. I was named for a contradiction: a Spartan general who had the mind of an Athenian. Like that man, I was born into something that is both mine and not-mine, a heritage of worldbreakers and tyrants. Seven hundred years after my ancestor Silenius au Lune conquered Earth, I was born the son of Brutus au

Arcos and Anastasia au Lune, heir to empire. Now that empire is a fractured, sick land so drunk on war and political upheaval it's likely to devour itself in my lifetime. But that is no longer my inheritance. When I was a boy, the day after the fall of House Lune, Cassius bent on a knee and told me his noble mission. "Gold forgot it was intended to shepherd, not rule. I reject my life and honor that duty: to protect the People. Will you join me?"

I had no family left. My home was at war. I was afraid. And, more than that, I wanted to be good. So I said yes and for the last ten years we have patrolled the fringes of civilization, protecting those who cannot protect themselves in the Reaper's new world. Roving between asteroids and backwater docks in the Asteroid Belt as the spheres change around us and war rages in the Core. Cassius brought us here in search of redemption, but no matter how many traders we save from pirates, or foundered ships we rescue, his eyes remain dark, and I still dream of the demons from my past.

I pull on a moth-eaten gray pullover and weave my way barefoot through the ship after Cassius, running my hands along the walls. "Hello, girl," I say. "You're sounding tired today." The *Archimedes* is an old fifty-meter Whisper-class corvette of the once-great Ganymede Dockyards, with three guns and engines fast enough to push her from Mars to the Belt in under four weeks at near-orbit. Shaped like a reared cobra head, she's made for scouting, raids. A hundred years ago she was top of the line, but she's seen better days. The larger part of my adolescent chores was scrubbing rust from the inside hull, oiling her gears, and patching her electrical innards.

But for all that tending, it's the *Archi*'s scars I love the most. Little beauty marks that make her our home. A dent under the kitchen's oven where Cassius fell and struck his head when drinking long ago—after news reached us of Darrow and Virginia's wedding. Charred ceiling panels made by the fire that Pytha started when she brought me a birthday pie when I was twelve and put the candles too close to a leaking oxygen pipe. Scratches on the walls of the razor training room. So many memories here woven together like those poems above my bed.

I enter the cozy, ovular cockpit. There is room for a pilot and two recessed seats for observation. Its original military lighting has been stripped out and replaced by warmer nodes. A thick Andalusian rug covers the floor. Several rows of mint and jasmine grow atop the console, presents I acquired for Pytha from a Violet's streetside botany shop in the Hanging Market on Ceres. Incense from the Erebian Mountains not far from Cassius's family home on Mars burns in the corner. Cassius and Pytha, our Blue pilot, peer out the cockpit windows.

Outside is the cargo hauler that drew us off our course to Lacrimosa Station. We were en route for ship repairs after last month's skirmish with Martian scar hunters when we received the distress signal from the Gulf between Republic space and Rim territory.

I told Cassius it was too dangerous to investigate so low on provisions.

But his heart guides us more than his head these days.

The ship out the viewport is a giant cube five hundred meters at the edge. Most of her decks are exposed to vacuum by design, while superstructure lattice holds together thousands of cargo containers. Her tag IDs her as the *Vindabona* out of the trade hub Ceres. She sits adrift and dark—a very odd, very dangerous thing in the Gulf. Several wild asteroids the size of cities float between us, ice crystals on their surfaces winking in the dark. We used one to mask our approach. The *Vindabona*'s civilian instruments would never detect a military ship like ours in this briar patch, but it's not the hauler that worries me. I scan the sensors for ghosts in the darkness.

"Well, she's a deepspace mulebitch, all right," Pytha murmurs in a monotone delivery that erodes punctuation and inflection. "Probably packing a hundred million credits of iron. Slag me but that's a crew I'd like to be on."

"Must you swear so early in the morning?" I ask.

"Shit, sorry, moon boy. Forgot to mind my fucking manners." Pytha is in her late fifties, with distant, pale blue eyes and skin the color of a walnut. Like all Blues, she still harbors the neurodevelopmental sculpting that enhances human-to-computer interaction but impairs communication outside her sect. She doesn't have the social niceties of the Palatine shuttle pilots.

My teacher grimaces. "Crew will make scratch," he says. "Captain might get a share to keep him loyal, but that's a hundred million credits of some trade lord's coin floating out there."

"A share, you say. What a novel idea for a captain to snag a share . . ." Pytha says.

"Pity you're a pilot and not a captain."

"Come now, Bellona. Between you and moon boy over here, you've got to have a dozen secret vaults. Why else do you think I signed up? Certainly wasn't your chiseled chin, *dominus*." She says the word sarcastically. "I'm sure you eagles have squirreled away some chit in hidden nests." Pytha snorts a strange little laugh to herself and looks back to the datastream as letters and symbols trickle past. The untrained ear would hear the Martian drawl in her voice and be done with it. But I catch the spice of Thessalonica, that city of grapes and duels that sprawls white and hot by Mars's Thermic Sea. Best known for the short tempers of its citizenry and the long list of deeds done by its most illustrious sons, the blackguard Brothers Rath.

That Thessalonican swagger is likely what got her expelled from the Midnight School and reduced to smuggling before her path crossed ours eight years ago. When Cassius learned she was Martian, he freed her from the brig of a mining city where she was imprisoned for a smuggling offense, and she's worked for us ever since. I've certainly learned new words since she came aboard.

Bald and barefoot, Pytha leans back in the pilot's chair, sipping coffee from the plastic dinosaur mug I won her in an arcade on Phobos years back. She's in gray cotton pants and wears her old sweatshirt. Her limbs are thin as a grasshopper's, the right bent under her, the left hanging off the side of the chair, which is shaped like half of a hard-boiled quail egg with the yolk scooped out. A second skin of stickers and decals from children's video games festoons its gray metal backside. The ship may belong to Cassius, but Pytha's left her mark.

"Sander, what do you think?" My teacher looks back at me.

I examine the ship out the viewport.

Cassius sighs. "Out loud."

"She's a VD Auroch-Z cosmosHauler. Fourth generation by my guess."

"Don't equivocate. We both know you're not guessing."

I wipe sleep from my eyes, annoyed. "She has 125 million cubic meters of hauling capacity. One main Gastron helium reactor. Built in the Venusian yards, circa 520 PCE. Crew of forty. One industrial docking bay. Two secondary tubes. Obviously she's a smuggler."

"Sounds like the human encyclopedia's got a turd up his nose," Pytha drawls. She pours a cup of coffee from her carafe and hands it back to me. I wish it were tea. "The last of the beans till we hit Lacrimosa. Sip wisely, peevish one."

I slip into the seat behind hers and take a mouthful of the coffee, wincing at the heat. "Apologies. I neglected to eat supper."

"I neglected to eat supper," Pytha repeats, mocking my accent. Born on the Palatine Hill of Luna, I have lamentably inherited the most egregiously stereotypical highLingo accents. Apparently others find it hilarious. "Haven't we servants to spoon-feed His Majesty supper?"

"Oh, shut your gory gob," I say, modulating my voice to mimic the Thessalonican bravado. "Better?"

"Eerily so."

"Skipping supper. No wonder you're a little twig," Cassius says, pinching my arm. "I daresay you don't even weigh a hundred ten kilos, my goodman."

"It's usable weight," I protest. "In any matter, I was reading." He looks at me blankly. "You have your priorities. I have mine, muscly creature. So piss off."

"When I was your age . . ."

"You despoiled half the women on Mars," I say. "And probably thought it was their honor. Yes, I'm aware. Forgive me, but I find books a passion more illuminating than carnivals of flesh."

He looks at me in amusement. "One day a woman is going to make a pretty meal of you."

"Spoken like a man who barely escaped the lion's jaws," I reply.

Pytha goes still and stares at Cassius for a long, awkward moment as her arithmetical brain endeavors in vain to divine whether he is offended or not. I sip my coffee again and nod to the ship. "To the matter, no legitimate Mars or Luna corp would send that poor girl out to the Gulf without escort. Not with Ascomanni about. Those

Julii-Barca Solar markings are false flags: wrong shade of red on that sun. Should be scarlet, but that there is vermilion. The Syndicate would know that. So, low-rate smugglers. Like Pytha said, probably hauling ore from some off-grid mine to avoid customs. And please, stop testing me, Cassius. At this point, you know that I know."

Cassius grunts, still stinging from the lion rejoinder. It was petty of me to say, and I feel lesser for having said it. Ten years recycling each other's air will make the best of men devils to one another. After all, that is why Blues were raised in sects.

"No bloody way that *vermilion* is an actual color," Pytha says.

Of course Pytha is as much an exile from her kind as we are from our own. I can't imagine why.

"Sounds more like the last name of a Silver," she adds. "Heh heh."

"Care to wager on that?" I ask gamely.

She ignores me. "Blackhell. You gotta be a special kind of stupid to wander into the Belt without legs to run or claws to fight. Nearest Republic gunship is ten million klicks away." She finishes her coffee and bites into the ion blueberry tail of a Cosmos Comet caffeine gummy. She offers me the remaining white tail, which I decline. "Suppose the distress signal was an accident? Didn't last long."

"Doubtful," Cassius replies.

It's too dark to tell if there are any carbon scoring markings along the outside of the *Vindabona*—the telltale sign of a forced breach. I don't find any, but that hardly disproves their existence. Pytha looks back at Cassius. "Do we risk hailing them?"

"Let's not announce ourselves just yet." Cassius looks back at me and speaks the word on both our minds: "Trap?"

"Perhaps." I overdo a nod to make up for my earlier barb. He doesn't seem sore. "Might be a pirate ship strapped to one of those asteroids. I daresay we've seen this one before. Emit a distress signal for bait, then sit back and wait. But . . . it's peculiar all the way out here. If it is a trap, it's a poorly conceived one. Who would run across it? No one likes the Gulf."

"So we should investigate." Cassius uses his instructor's voice.

"With caution," I confirm. "There may be souls aboard. But we needn't risk the *Archi* just yet."

"My mind exactly. So what do we do, my goodman?"

I smile and put down my coffee. "Well, Cassius, I daresay we should put on our dancing shoes."

Cassius and I float through space toward an oblong asteroid. It rotates lazily in the darkness. Veins of ice glitter and wind through her craggy skin as we coast into a rock formation at the edge of a shadowy canyon large enough to swallow the Citadel of Light. We arrest our motion on a jagged scree. My breath echoes in my ears. Darkness stretches under me, plunging into the fathomless depths of the asteroid. I doubt very much any man has ever set foot upon this cold chunk of rock, much less looked into its bowels. I feel it's my duty to give in to temptation and shine a light down into the canyon. I flick the switch on my forearm and a beam of light cuts into the darkness and is devoured by the lower reaches. There is no bottom that my eye can see. But at least now a man's eye has seen that.

"Turn that off," Cassius orders over the com.

"Apologies. Was looking for space worms."

"Biologically absurd," Pytha mutters from the cockpit. *"Organic tissue must have calories. What would they eat?"*

"Spacemen," I say with a smile.

"Spaceboys," Cassius corrects.

I'm certain that, had I been born in a different time, I would have been an explorer. Since I was a boy, I've had an insatiable itch for things remote and unknown. In the Citadel, I dreamed of sailing the violent light of distant nebulas and charting astral seas. The great philosopher Sagan once preached it was in our nature as a species to explore. Despite the modern chaos, we do live in a new age of innovation. Perhaps some brilliant boy or girl who has yet to take their first step will one day make an engine to carry us faster than the speed of light beyond our single star. Beyond the stain of man. Would all this chaos be worth that one innovation?

I often imagine what humans could do if there were no scarcity. Nothing to fight over. Just an unending expanse to explore and name and fill with life and art. I smile at the pleasant fiction. A man can dream.

Not wanting to bring the *Archimedes* into a trap, Cassius and I pushed away from her airlock toward the nearest asteroid in our EVO suits fifteen minutes ago. Now we reorient ourselves and push off again toward the hulking *Vindabona.* Rows and rows of cargo containers drift suspended between metal beams, bound together by wires and mesh netting.

Cassius and I use our shoulder thrusters to slow our approach, settling into the floating carbon mesh that pins in a row of green crates. They're stamped with Republic stars. With Pytha guiding us over the coms, we pull ourselves along the outside of the ship toward the central service airlock. There, I unscrew the paneling on the door's locking mechanism and hijack the console till the orange doors open silently. Cassius and I drift into the airlock. The outer door closes behind us. We each grip the metal rungs inside. Red light throbs down from the ceiling as the airlock finishes its cycle. Pressure slowly pumps into the room. Then oxygen. Finally the pull of gravity. We remove our razors from their holsters on our hips. A pair of lazy silver tongues of metal float in the air, two meters long, stiffening to just over a meter of sword as we toggle them to their rigid state. His is straight. I prefer mine in the slight crescent of my house. The red light becomes green and the interior door of the airlock opens with an asthmatic gasp. As ever, Cassius makes sure he's the first through before glancing back to make sure I follow.

The repair bay is empty except for tools and ancient EVO suits hanging from hooks. Pale lights embedded in the gray ceiling flicker, hurling shadows about the room. An indicator blinks green and so I retract my helm into a small compartment at the back of the neck and breathe in the scent of cleaning solution and oil. Reminds me of my early days with Cassius, hiding out in backwater transportation hubs, searching for a ship to carry us away from Luna. Away from the Rising.

That was a lonely time. The better part of me felt carved away as we fled Luna and I knew I would never again hear my grandmother say my name, never follow Aja along the garden paths to train before the morning pachelbel birds even woke. All the people who had ever loved me were gone.

I was alone. And not just alone, but hunted. I shove the memories in the void where my grandmother taught me to stow them lest they overwhelm me like they did her when she was a girl.

"Eagle to Mother Hen, we're inside. Level sixteen. No signs of life," Cassius says.

"Copy, Eagle. Do try to use words first this time instead of blades?"

"Unlike certain pilots I know, I have impeccable manners, Mother Hen."

"Captain," she stresses. *"Call me Captain."*

"As you say, pilot." Cassius lets his helmet retract and winks at me. His face is harder than when we first met. But every now and again there's that twinkle in his eyes, like a light inside a far-off tent, making you feel warm even though you're still outside. And I am outside. He thinks I don't see how wounded he is. How I'm a replacement for the brother Darrow of Lykos took from him in the Institute. Sometimes he looks at me and I know he sees Julian.

A small, selfish part of me wishes he just saw me.

I follow Cassius into the hall. The ship is barren and gripped by silence. Something here is amiss. Quietly we make our way through the ship, but before we've gone long, we find a smear of blood on the floor leading from a side passage to a central lift. We trace the blood to the starboard escape pod bay, and there, before the large doors, we find a massacre.

Gore congeals on the walls. Bodily fluids pool on the dented floor. The whole room redolent with the tangy scent of iron and sick, so much so that I would gag were I not conscious of Cassius's eyes on me. Red handprints streak the escape pod door, as if men were trying to claw their way out. Yet there are no bodies. I focus and try to view the room with the Mind's Eye—removed, analytical, as my grandmother trained me.

"The crew was killed here. Under a day ago," I say, examining the state of the blood. When I was a boy, my grandmother had Securitas investigators take me to murder scenes in Hyperion City to teach me the barbarism under the surface of civilization, under the manners of men. I bend on a knee and begin processing the scene. "Judging from the blood spatters, I would postulate that there were two assailants. Men or women of our size or larger, judging by their bootprints. No blast scoring or char indicates the work was done with blades . . . and hammers."

"Ascomanni," Cassius says darkly.

"Evidence suggests it." I take a sample of the blood on my finger and wipe it on the datapad built into a socket on my EVO suit's left forearm. "Brown, Red, and Blue DNA markers. Our smugglers. Several were killed and then dragged out. Others were still alive."

"You watching, Pytha?" Cassius asks.

"Yes," she says quietly over the com. Our suits feed her visuals as well. She's more sensitive to violence than we are. *"No sign of ship signatures from the Gulf. But if it's all the same, will you please hurry it up? I've got an itch about this."*

As do I.

The term *Ascomanni* is derived from the Germanic for "Ash Men." The first Vikings sailed down European rivers in boats of ash wood. And ash is what they left behind.

Once, the Ascomanni were just deepspace legends, dark whispers passed by traders and smugglers to new recruits in the shadowy hollows of asteroid cantinas or docking-bay watering holes. In the deep of space, so they'd say, there lurked Obsidian tribes who escaped the Society's culling of the rest of their race following the Dark Revolt hundreds of years ago. Hunted by my family's extermination squads and Olympic Knights, they fled into the darkness. For years they plagued the far colonies of Neptune and Pluto, remaining little more than myth to the Core.

But now, with the Obsidian diaspora from the poles of Earth and Mars, that myth has become reality. Bands of Obsidians, alienated by the new strange world, freed from military slavery to Gold masters—or exhausted from the Reaper's war—embrace the legend of their ancestors.

They've not so much left the Ice as they've brought the Ice to the stars.

Inside the lift where the blood trail ends, viscera smear the button for the thirteenth deck. Cassius presses it with the hilt of his razor. I feel the righteous anger building in my friend as we rise. It infects me.

The lift wheezes to a stop, shuddering as the doors part and reveal the hall leading into the thirteenth floor of the old vessel. Cheap white lights burn down at derelict halls, casting wicked, sharp shadows. Air ventilators with clogged purifiers rattle in the ceiling. Down the center of the hall, a red trail bifurcates the rusted metal flooring. Handprints smear the ground to either side of the trail like crimson butterfly wings. Cassius leads and I follow the trail, our razors held behind us at a diagonal as Aja taught us, our aegis arms held before us, bracers cold and inert but ready to spring into a meter-square energy shield at a moment's notice. My new plasma pistol is light against my right thigh.

Faded yellow signs on the walls indicate washrooms and crew quarters. We check the rooms as we go. The first several are abandoned. Unmade beds and overturned pictures and chairs remain as evidence of violence. The crew was caught sleeping.

Inside the next room, we find what's left of the crew. Corpses have been stacked in a heap against the far wall. A stagnant pool of blood expands from the pile and in it I see the reflection of a single terrified eye. I rush to the pile and pull the dead to the side to find six shivering survivors beneath the corpses. They're bound and beaten and tied feet to hands. I bend to free them but they flinch away, making inhuman, squealing sounds. Cassius bends to a knee and removes his right gauntlet so they can see the Gold Sigils on his hand.

"Salve," he says in a deep voice. The prisoners calm, the sign bringing them courage. "*Salve,* friends," he says as their eyes search his face and see the Peerless scar there. A scar I've never earned.

"Dominus . . ." they murmur, weeping. *"Dominus . . ."*

"Peace. We've come to help you," I say as I ungag a paunchy Red man. One of his eyes is swollen shut from a gash at the eyebrow. He smells like urine. "How many are there?" I ask. His crooked teeth chatter together so terribly he cannot even utter a single word. I wonder if he's ever spoken to a Gold. I feel such pity for him. I rest a hand on his shoulder, intending to comfort him. He flinches back. "Goodman, *salve*. Peace," I say softly. "You are safe now. We have come to help. Tell me how many there are."

"Fifteen . . . maybe more, *dominus* . . ." he whispers in a thick Phobosian accent, fighting back tears. I look over at Cassius. Fifteen is too many without our pulseArmor. "Leader is . . . on . . . on . . . the bridge with the captain. Are you Moon Lords?"

"How did they board you?" I ask, ignoring his question. "Do they have a vessel?"

He nods. "Came from the asteroids, they did. Therix—our helmsman—fell asleep uplinked. Drunk." He shudders. "We woke and . . . we woke and they were in the halls. Tried to run. To get to escape pods. They punished us. . . ." His crooked teeth chatter together. I'm so close I can see the blackheads on his bulbous nose. The veins on his neck stand out from fluid redistribution from extended travel in low gravity. He's pallid and weak in the bones. I wager it's been half a life since he's felt the sun's warmth. "Their ship boarded through the cargo hangar."

"Explains why we couldn't see it," I say to Cassius.

He ignores me. "Why are you so far out here with full freight?" he asks the man.

"Shouldn't have been . . . shouldn't have taken the money."

"The money from whom?" I ask.

"The passenger. The Gold."

Cassius and I exchange a glance. "There's a Gold on board?" he asks. "Did they have a scar?"

"Not Peerless." The Red shakes his head, and Cassius breathes a small sigh of relief. "She came to the captain on Psyche. Paid us to . . ." He swallows, glancing over our shoulders as if expecting an Obsidian to appear there. "She paid us to drop her at an asteroid . . . S-1392."

"That's near the edge of the Gulf," I say. "Just outside Rim territory."

"Yeah. Captain told her nothin' was there, but she paid as much as our freight. Told him we shouldn't get involved with Golds. But he didn't listen. He never listens. . . ."

"Did she give a name?" Cassius asks.

"No name." The man shakes his head. "But she sounded like him." He points at me, and I know Cassius has the same thought. Are the Obsidians here for the ship or the Gold?

"They might not be Ascomanni," I say. "Could be the Rising."

"Darrow wouldn't massacre civilians."

"In this war, two-thirds of the dead are civilians," I say sharply. "Have you forgotten the Sack of Luna by Sefi's Horde?"

"Not at all. Nor have I forgotten New Thebes," Cassius replies, referring to when my godfather, the Ash Lord, orbitally bombarded one of Mars's great cities after she fell to the Rising.

"Boys," Pytha's voice crackles in our ears, cutting through the tension between us. *"Boys, we have company."*

"How many?" Cassius asks.

"Three ships inbound."

I stand. "Three?"

"How the goryhell are you just telling us?" Cassius snaps.

"Couldn't pick them up because of the asteroid interference. They must have called in more of them to haul in the Vindabona.*"*

The crewmembers sense our unease and begin to shudder again in fear.

"What grade?" I ask.

"Military, third class. Two four-gun lancers, and an eight-gun Storm-class corvette. They're Ascomanni."

"How can you tell?" I ask.

"They have bodies on their hulls."

"It's a gorydamn hunting party." Cassius curses quietly. We could go toe to toe with one of the lancers, but a Storm-class corvette would rip *Archi* to shreds. "How long do we have?"

"Five minutes. Haven't yet spotted me. I suggest you get off that heap."

I rush to cut the remaining restraints off the prisoners. "Hen, I need you to pop off that asteroid and burn for the *Vindabona*'s transfer tube," Cassius says. "We have people to evacuate."

"They'll see me if I make an approach," Pytha says.

"They might have guns, but we've got engines," Cassius replies.

"Copy."

"Can you all run?" Cassius asks the crew. They stare up at him without answering. "Well, you're going to have to. The Obsidians are still out there. You see them, you keep it together and get to the tube. Let us fight. You obey everything I say or I leave you to die. I need you to nod." They do. "Good."

"What about the Gold?" I ask Cassius. "They could still be alive."

"You heard Pytha," he replies. "We don't have time."

"I won't leave someone behind for those barbarians to keep. Especially not one of us. It is not honorable."

"I said no," Cassius snaps, almost using my name in front of the smugglers. "It's not worth the risk of all their lives for one person." He surveys the wobbling crew before us. "Everyone quiet. Stay together. Now follow me." Cassius, as always, is first out the door before I can reply.

The prisoners follow quick as they can into the hall back the way we came. I guard the rear, helping along a limping Brown. The bone of his right arm sticks out of a tear in his green jumpsuit. Cassius looks back to make sure I'm keeping pace. We load into the lift we rode up on to take it back down to the third level. But as the doors begin to close, I jump off the lift without a glance back at Cassius.

"Dammit, boy," Cassius says over the com after the doors seal and the lift carries downward. *"What do you think you're doing?"*

"What Lorn would do," I reply, walking back the way we came. He says we don't have time, but I know how careful he is with me, how cautiously he guards my life. "I'll be sensible. Make a quick reconnoiter."

He's quiet for a moment, and I know he's reserving his condemnation for later. *"Hurry, but watch your tail."*

"Naturally."

I adjust my hand on my razor and move back down the hall. I take efforts to calm my breath, but every corner I turn I expect to see a savage waiting with bloody teeth and hollow eyes. I feel the fear and remember my grandmother's words. "Do not let fear touch you. Fear is the torrent. The raging river. To fight it is to break and drown. But to stand astride it is to see it, feel it, and use its course for your own whims."

I am the master of my fear. I let myself sink into the Mind's Eye.

My breathing slows. A cold, distant clarity settles over me. I hear the rattle of air purifiers clogged by dust, the pulse of generators vibrating through the metal floor into my boots.

And then I hear them.

The low, quiet rumble of their voices drifts down the dark metal hall like a grumbling glacier. My hands sweat inside my gloves. Everything Aja and Cassius taught me seems so distant now as the metal grating underneath my boots creaks. I've killed Ascomanni before, but never by myself.

At the end of the hall, I peer around the corner. I don't see the Obsidians. The commissary is round and holds several tables, the centermost of which has been laden with mounds of clothing. I'm about to move into the room when the mound moves and I realize my mistake. Three Ascomanni sit at the center table. Their long, braided hair cascades white and dirty down broad backs. Pale, scarred skin peeks out from under scrap armor. They speak in *nagal* and are hunched together eating and drinking the foodstores from the ship. Revulsion and fear swirl together in the pit of my belly.

Be the calm.

I lean back behind the wall and listen to their conversation. The savages' accents are thick, their voices sluggish and drunken. From Earth's North Pole. One criticizes the flavor of the man meat and longs to eat fresh elk. His friend says something I do not understand. Something about the Ice. Another is irritated that she claimed no slaves in the taking of the ship. She asks if she could buy the Sunborn from the first. He laughs at her with his mouth full and says she belongs to their jarl, body and meat. The Sunborn; the Gold.

I expect Lorn would kill them. My own pride would see me do the same, to prove to myself that I am greater than the fear I now feel. But pride is a vanity I cannot afford. My grandmother's lessons win out. Why fight when you can maneuver? I find a way around the commissary and continue my search, listening for any sound of life.

My pre-allotted time ticks away. I'll have to double back in two minutes. There's nothing but the Obsidian voices echoing down the halls and the unhappy rattle of distant generators. Then . . . I hear something. A faint creaking from behind a bulkhead. I find the door and clasp the narrow handle. It opens slowly, sliding back into its frame and squealing as it goes. I wince, praying to Jove that no one heard. I wait, poised with my razor in the hall for the Obsidians to come running. None do. I slip into the room.

It is filled with the rest of the crew. They litter the floor in mesh cages that constrict around their bodies. All lowColors. And hanging above them from the dark room's ceiling is a thin wire net that's been looped around a gas pipe. It sways back and forth and inside it, hanging upside down as the wire cuts into her bare skin, is the body of a naked woman with Gold Sigils upon the backs of her hands.

9

LYSANDER

The Passenger

I RUSH FIRST TO THE GOLD.

Her body is contorted and twisted inside the confines of her prison. A bent metal chair lies beneath her, having been used to beat her as she hung in the net. Her right hand is a charred, burned mess from the welding torch that sits on a table. Blood seeps there, dripping onto the floor. The smell of burned skin and hair claws into my nostrils, making my eyes water.

She's dead. She has to be.

"Help us!" a Red woman whispers out of a bloody mouth. *"Dominus . . ."*

"Quiet," I snap, glancing back at the door. Dozens of pairs of eyes stare out at me from behind the cages. Each prisoner pleading with me.

I creep closer to the Gold, and as I reach to touch the net, her eyes flash open in the low light. Goryhell. I almost fall down. She's alive. Black engine oil has been slathered over her body, along with fouler-smelling things.

"Dominus . . ." a Brown hisses.

"Salve," I say to the Gold in a Thessalonican drawl. "I'm here to

help. My name is Castor au Janus." She watches me without speaking, giving no sign that she even understands. "I'm going to help you out, but you have to be quiet and quick. The Ascomanni are still outside. Do you understand?"

"Yes, I understand," she says. Hers is a rich Palatine accent. It startles me. The man was right. She's from the Luna courts as well. What is she doing all the way out here?

"Stay very still," I say. I stand beneath the net and slide my razor across the steel cable, cutting it from the ceiling. The girl falls into my arms. I expected her to lash out, but she stays still within the tight mesh. I see now how deeply the tacNet's cut into her skin. TacNets, or birdcages, are fired from compressed fiber cartridges and designed for police forces to engulf and constrict around a prisoner to harmlessly subdue them. But if you toggle with the contraction restrictions, you can eviscerate a prisoner to death. I set the woman on the ground and cut the wires one by one until she's able to crawl free. She lies there naked stretching her joints, teeth chattering with the pain.

I realize now that she's young, maybe even younger than my twenty years. I feel an overwhelming urge to protect her. I cover her body with a plastic tool sheet.

"It is well," I say. "You're safe now." I stand to go help the others.

"Stims," she manages through her chattering teeth. "Need stims."

I bend back down and produce a syringe from the dispenser on the right thigh of my EVO suit. It's one of my last. She snatches it from my hand and stabs it into the bicep of the burned limb. Her body convulses as the drug rushes through her system. She sighs with pleasure. "More," she demands. I glance at the other prisoners and produce my last two. She shocks me by injecting both at the same time. It's too much for her body mass unless she's built up a resistance to them, which inherently means something dangerous. There's something wrong here.

Filled with a manic energy from the stims, she stumbles to her feet. I spring back to catch her from falling, but she steadies herself using the table.

"We must leave," I say softly to the girl. "More Ascomanni are coming. We have to be gone before their ships dock. Help me with the others." Nodding along, she finds her clothing in a pile on the floor near the door. Still covered in oil, she dons the pants and a green jacket, fumbling with the zipper because of the drugs in her system.

"Sander," Cassius says in my ear as I bend to cut the Red woman from her cage with my razor. *"What's your status?"*

"I found the Gold, Regulus." I patch him to my visual feed.

"Copy." He pauses, seeing the others. *"Lysander . . ."*

"Boy," the Gold says from behind me. I turn. She's less than an arm's length away. "What docking tube are you using?"

"Two-B."

"Two-B?" She nods more to herself than to me. "I'll return it to you in four minutes. On my honor."

"Return what?"

There's a blur. I don't even see her strike as the meat of her palm collides with the side of my temple. I stumble, and something, maybe her elbow or knee, slams into my opposite ear and I go down, seeing stars. There's pressure on my hip, and I hear her footsteps going out the door. She's four seconds gone before I realize what she took. My razor. The one Cassius gave me on my sixteenth birthday. The one that belonged to Karnus. Its custom Bellona hilt is covered by a plain metal shell, but to Cassius it is priceless. Dazed, I lunge after her into the hallway. My legs go like rubber and I almost fall.

The lowColors shout in fear, terrified that I'm going to abandon them. I lunge back toward their cages, but I don't have anything to cut with. I can't use my plasma pistol. The wire is too tight to their bodies. Panic threatens to grip me. I tug on the severed strands of the Red woman's cage. *"Lysander . . ."* Cassius says. The lowColors are clamoring now, rolling around on the floor. *"It's too late."* I pull as hard as I can. The fiberwire of the net slices through my gloves and into my skin. Blood wells against the wire. *"Lysander! You have to leave them."*

"No, I can help them. . . ."

I groan as I pull with all my strength at the wire, using my legs as leverage. The wire cuts my fingers to the bone. And it doesn't even fray. There's a scream from the lowColors. I wheel around and see an Obsidian at the door. I grab my pistol and fire clumsily. The plasma bolt takes the Obsidian's head off from the nose up. Another one fills the frame. I fire and he ducks back into the hall.

"Lysander, get out of there!" Cassius says.

A scream wells up inside, but doesn't escape my lips. I stare down at the wailing lowColors, at the mothers and fathers I could have freed, their cries puncturing my fantasy of heroism and honor. They thrash on the floor screaming at me to save them, but I can't. The Obsidian death warble echoes down the hall.

Fear has come.

I run like a coward. Back into the hall, firing around the corner blindly. The Obsidian's chest melts inward as he swings his axe. I bend under it and slam into the far wall, where I use the impact to push off and struggle to my feet. The Obsidian's chest is burned through to the liver, but he stumbles toward me—a tower of sinewy muscle and scrap armor and the pelts of dead animals. Aja and Cassius both told me never to come within arm's reach of an Obsidian. They alone can break the reinforced bones of my kind. But there's no other choice. He swings his axe again, and I charge inside the blow, hitting the inside of his axe arm with the point of my elbow, jamming the point into his brachial artery. His arm goes limp, but the force of the collision knocks me sideways. I use the momentum to flow left, and drive my right knee into the genicular artery on the inside of his leg. He roars in pain and charges straight into me, slamming me against the wall. It's like the time I was kicked by one of Virginia's stallions. The breath goes out of me. His right hand grabs my throat and lifts me up against the wall, straining to crush my trachea. Cartilage crackles. I lower my jaw against his grip, but the world's going black. Bits of meat cling to his beard. The rancid smell of rotting teeth fills my nose. Twisting my body, I pull twice on the trigger of my pistol. The plasma enters under his rib cage at an angle and burns through his heart. His eyes go wide with shock and his body collapses, dead. I land and suck in air just in time to see the third Obsidian raging toward me down the hall.

I fire, miss, and run.

Darkened hallways and empty rooms flash past. I heave myself around them, gripping girders to tighten my turns around corners.

"The Ascomanni corvette's docked on 1C," Pytha says. *"Dead ahead."*

I skid to a halt. I hear them ahead of me, their tribal voices echoing as they move into the ship through the transfer causeways. Their boots rattle the metal. Each half again my weight, maybe more. They'll cut off the route to the lift. I turn back the way I came, checking my gun's display. The energy cartridge has seventeen pulls in it. I feel naked without my razor. But fighting isn't the answer today.

"Pytha. Hallway to lift 11A is closed. I need you to guide me."

"Take your next left," she says without missing a beat. Conscious that Cassius is listening, judging, I take the left. *"Two hundred meters."* I dash the distance, slow in my EVO suit. *"Maintenance lift is on your second right."*

I reach the lift and press the call button. It doesn't respond. A little sign's been affixed to the door itself, apologizing rather crudely for the broken lift by means of a talking phallus. "Lift's out," I say, making efforts to measure my breathing.

"Back twenty meters, left, stairs are right there. Twenty down."

"Back?" I ask, hoping I heard wrong.

"Now!"

I backtrack without running into the Obsidian and find the stairs to begin my descent. Two levels down the stairwell, I pause. I hear them. Their boots beat the stairs two levels above me. Through the metal grating I see their dark shapes, their milk-pale hair. The chant, called the khoomei, groans through the hall. It is a plea to Hel, Obsidian goddess of death, to receive her offerings. I clear the whole next flight of stairs with a single jump, racing down the levels as fast as I can. Behind me, like a dark avalanche, gaining, rumbling, and threatening to swallow me up, rush the raiders. Can't see their numbers. Can't hear what Pytha and Cassius are saying. My body is distant and numb and my mind still and focused.

I lose my footing on a rusted stair and nearly fall as the weight of the suit pulls me toward the ground. I stumble up, firing two quick shots with my pistol. I score a lucky hit. Someone grunts and a shadow of blood sprays on the wall as the green energy bolts hit meat, giving me time to reach the docking level.

I race through the metal door and close it behind me, cranking on the hatch as hard as I can to seal it. But the wheel stops and then turns against me as someone stronger on the other side begins to open it. I backpedal and fire three shots into the hatch, turning the metal wheel into red-hot slag and jamming the door. The muscle fibers of my arm tremble from the pistol's recoil. They'll be through the door in a moment, but I bought myself precious seconds.

"Hundred meters straight. Fifth left. Straight twenty meters. First right."

I follow Pytha's instructions, but as I turn to flee the door, I slam into someone and we both go down, hard. I roll as I fall and aim my pistol back up at my assailant. But it's not an Obsidian. It's the Gold girl. She's limping to her feet, bearing half a dozen new wounds on her oil-slick skin. Her jacket is in tatters. She carries my razor in her hand. It is bloody to the hilt. Clumps of white hair cling to the gore.

How she is standing is a miracle. At her stomach, layers of skin and fat pull back along a six-inch gash to the right of the belly button. Looks like an axe wound. She hunches there, listening to the Obsidians hammering on the door.

"Give me my razor," I say.

"Move." She lunges toward the door with her razor and sticks it through the molten metal. A raider on the other side screams and she draws the razor back. Blood hisses as the molten metal turns it to vapor.

"Where's your ship?" she asks, turning on me with wild, incandescent eyes. The door wheezes as the Obsidians knock half of it off its hinges. "Where is your gorydamn ship?" The Luna accent falters under the adrenaline in her voice, replaced by something very different. The wound in her gut is leaking blood badly.

"This way." I move to help her walk, but she flinches away. "Don't be a fool. You can barely stand," I say. Glancing back at the bending door, she relents with a hiss of air between her teeth and throws her arm around mine. We hobble fast as we can, putting the door behind us, passing through the cargo level, containers and cranes to every side.

We take a right. Cassius stands guarding the interior of the transfer bridge that connects our ship to the *Vindabona,* clad in his EVO suit and helm. He fires his pulseRifle over our heads at the pack that rounds the corner behind us. The distorted energy screams past my ears. There's a howl. I glance back and see an Obsidian's head disappear, neck spouting blood. Magnetically shot bolts as long as my forearm rip past us and embed themselves into walls. Then we're past Cassius and stumbling into the narrow causeway. He follows behind me, his pulseRifle roaring as he unloads the last of its battery into an Obsidian warrior who jumps into the causeway after us. The man's torso tears in half and spins backward, leaving his legs behind on the causeway. Cassius kicks the legs off the ship.

"Disengage!" he shouts to Pytha. Our bulkhead door seals, closing off the causeway as I spill with the Gold girl to the transfer bay floor inside the *Archimedes,* panting and soaked with sweat and blood. The girl leans her forehead against the metal floor and coughs in pain. Pytha pulls an emergency disengage from the *Vindabona* and we bank away. Cassius stares down at me. I feel his rage, despite his helm's smooth visage.

There's silence except for weeping from the crew we rescued. They're sprawled like us on the floor, huddled together, some in exaltation, others still in fear, not yet believing that they could possibly be safe. They're not.

"You idiot," Cassius says down at me. "What the hell were you thinking?" Before I can answer, he kicks my razor from the Gold's hands. He bends, as if to grab her face to look for the dread mark on her cheek, when the floor of the *Archi* opens up between us. He twists back and away as a fist-sized gray blur shrieks through and then goes out through the ceiling with a monstrous gasp of air. A hole has been ripped in the ship. Depressurization sirens scream. Red pulses from the overhead lights. Another railgun slug pierces our hull, slamming through the floor up through the body of the paunchy Red man we rescued, spraying us with his blood. Pytha shouts something in our coms. Pressure screams out of the holes. Then the cellular armor slides over the external damage and the mad gout of air stops. The sirens cease their wailing, but the warning lights continue to throb.

"Our engines are hit," Pytha says. *"Number one is at half power. Shunting energy from it to the shields."*

Cassius gestures to the gash on the Gold girl's stomach. "Cauterize that or she'll bleed out." He rushes through the survivors of the crew to the bridge. The Gold girl is losing too much blood. Her skin is pale under the black oil and her chest rises and falls with shallow rapidity. I lift her arm to get her to the infirmary, but she's too weak. The stims have overloaded her system. Her legs go out, so I loop my arm behind her knees and my other around her back and carry her through the narrow halls. The fierce face she wore when I first found her is gone. She's quiet and still, her eyes watching me, so distant from the chaos around us. I lay her down on the medical bed as the *Archi*'s guns fire. The infirmary is small and understocked. Syringes tremble in their cases as we take another hit.

Those screaming faces of the lowColors.

The wails still chase me.

They'll all die.

The girl watches as I cut open her soiled shirt with medical shears. Two minor lacerations rend her skin above her breasts. My main concern is the axe wound. It's a deep and angry gouge six inches long in her lower left abdomen. What was she thinking, going back? What could have been so important? I clean the wound with an antibac spray and use the hospital-grade medical scanner to inspect her organs for damage. Her liver is lacerated. She'll need a real surgeon, and soon. All I can do here is cauterize the capillaries and load her with bloodsim. Flesh sizzles under the laser. She groans in pain. Once it's sealed, I apply a layer of resFlesh and strap on a compression pack. The ship shudders.

"Who are you?" I ask the girl. "What's your name?"

She does not answer as her eyes drift closed. "S-1392," she whispers. *"Help . . . at . . . S-1392."* Her words trail away as she falls unconscious.

S-1392 is the asteroid she was heading toward. But what did she mean by "help"?

I examine her as if her face will hold the answers. The lashes of her eyes are longer than I might have expected. But even with the smear of blood and oil, I can see the stringy muscles of a fighter and a testament of old scars upon her skin. Too many for her young age. I trace my fingers over the six parallel scars that rake her lower back. Accompanying those scars are two old knife wounds near her heart, a terrible burn on her left arm, and the remnants of an old wound on the left side of her head that claimed the top corner of her ear. I thought of her as a girl when I found her in that cage. But she's not a girl. She's a predator in young skin. Who else would go back into that nightmare ship?

Why did you have to take my razor?

Did she leave something behind? I search her clothes, her body. There's nothing hidden. No false teeth. But I have a suspicion. I run my hand over her face. The cheekbones are bold and high and covered like the rest of her face with oil. I scrape my nails along her closed eyelids. The false lashes there are well made and applied with some sort of resin. My fingers drift to her right cheek. Dread twists my belly as I feel the skin there give.

I stand up and away.

I know what she is.

I suspected when she stole my razor, and then when her voice broke from the accent of the Palatine. Was she affecting that one? Was it a guise? I pick the corner of the odd patch of skin on her face till a thin layer of resFlesh—the same sort Cassius uses to disguise himself—pulls away from the cheek, revealing what lies beneath. Along her right cheekbone, slashing through the black oil at a cruel angle, is the pale mark of a Peerless Scarred.

10

DARROW

Liberty Eternal

SEVRO SQUIRMS ON THE WHITE CUSHION next to me as Publius cu Caraval, the Copper Tribune, leader of the Copper bloc, finishes the roll call. He's an elegant firebrand of a man. Middle-aged, small of stature, with a narrow, pleasant face, a large nose, cold eyes, and an ambivalence toward fashion that borders on antagonism. When he's not in his toga, he still wears the same drab suits he did as a public lowColor defense lawyer before the war. Since then, he's risen to become a voice of reason in the divided Senate, and an occasional ally of my wife's. They call him the Incorruptible for his punctilious nature and lack of vices.

Caraval stands on a small circular plinth before the tiered C-shaped marble steps that encircle the white and red porphyry floor. Small wooden chairs are set for each senator on the steps. Behind Caraval, recessed from the plinth, squats the unadorned Morning Chair of the Sovereign. Made of whitewood carved with simple geometric designs, the chair looks dreadfully uncomfortable and is without cushion—Mustang had it removed. She leans against one of the arms of the chair and watches the senators. They sit clustered by Color and political affiliation upon the cushioned steps—Dancer's Vox Populi to the left of the huge Liberty Doors that lead out of the Forum to the steps and the Via Triumphia. Mustang's Optimates sit to the right. Obsidian and Copper centrists occupy the middle.

Bored by the formality, Sevro lounges beside me in crisp military whites. He's staring at the ceiling, infatuated by the mural there. It is a romantic rendering of the Phobos Address, my speech that launched the Rising on Phobos ten years ago. I look young and radiant in paints of gold and scarlet and float on gravBoots, cape billowing behind me like a magenta storm cloud, flanked by Howlers, the Sons of Ares, and Ragnar, even though he wasn't exactly there. Sevro's jaw clenches.

"That doesn't look anything like me." He nods to his own image. He's right. The eyes of the rendering are blood-red and insane. His hair's standing on end. His teeth look like rows of shattered porcelain. "You look like a bloody saint plowed an angel and out you popped. I look like a deranged fucking mutant that eats babies."

I pat Sevro on the leg. Mustang catches my eye and nods up to the last of the Red Senators who have just entered the room. Dancer shuffles along at the head of the procession of my people to their seats. He feels my eyes and meets them without a smile. Even knowing he's my adversary of the day, it's hard not to feel fondness for him.

With the roll call finalized, I turn my attention to Mustang.

"A quorum being present, the floor will now hear the scheduled petition." She looks to me. "ArchImperator."

The sound of my boots on stone echoes through the Senate chamber as I go to take my place on the plinth facing the senators. I spy Daxo, who sits surrounded by his fellow Gold senators on the far right. He looks like a statue of some pagan god in repose, though I know he's still nursing as monstrous a hangover as I am. Only when the tension has reached its pinnacle do I finally speak.

"Mercury . . . is liberated."

The right half of the senators, along with the Coppers, led smoothly by Caraval, roar their approval.

"The First Fleet of the Republic under the command of Imperator Orion xe Aquarii met that of the Ash Lord over Mercury while the Second Fleet under my personal command launched an Iron Rain against the continent of Borealis. Through high cost, we prevailed." The highColor senators lead the room to their feet yet again, roaring their fanatical support for the war effort. The Vox Populi remain silent. And so, I notice, do the Obsidians.

"Now the Ash Lord is in retreat. He has recalled the greater sum of his forces to make a final stand at Venus. But soon we will follow. Brothers and sisters, we stand upon the threshold of victory."

It is a full minute before the renewed applause dies down.

"But we yet have a choice to make." I take my time, allowing the silence to grow again. "Do we allow this war to linger? To consume another generation of our young? Or do we press the enemy and grind them until the last of the chains have been shattered?" I speak over the applause this time, letting the fervor spread through me. "It has been a decade of war. But we can end it here. Now." I spare a look up to the viewing deck above, where the holonetworks have their cameras. My enemy will be watching this later with his daughter and advisors, his nimble mind dissecting my words, divining my plans based on the response of these senators. But more importantly, he'll be watching me. He must not see my exhaustion. Mercury was a great victory. We robbed him the Iron of his docks. But Venus . . . Venus is the prize.

Even here, amidst the thunderous applause of the right, I hear Lorn's words echo in the dark place of my mind.

Death begets death begets death.

"Brothers and sisters of the Republic, we are one choice away from a fully liberated Core. A free System from Sol to the asteroid belt. We would be the first men and women to ever see it. But it will be a sight not without cost." I pause and permit, for one small moment, the weight of these last years to show on my face. "Like you, I wish for nothing more than peace. I wish for a world where the machine of war does not swallow our young." I look to my wife. "I wish to live in a world where my child can choose his own destiny, where the sins of the past do not define the nature of his life as it has defined all of ours. Our enemies have held dominion over us for too long. First as slaves, then adversaries. And what stability, what harmony can we bring to the worlds we have freed while they continue to define us?

For the sake of our brothers and sisters on Venus and Mercury . . ." I look to Dancer. ". . . for the sake of the souls we have unchained, for the sake of our children, give me the tools and I will finish this war, once and for all."

They roar in approval.

I look to Daxo and, as we agreed, he stands to tower over his fellow senators.

"My noble friends . . ." His large hands splay plaintively outward. "I know you are weary. I feel the years of war in my bones too. I believe I had hair when this all began." There's laughter. "I know better than you the heart of the Peerless Scarred. They do not have the spirit for peace. It is not in their nature to accept this new world we have made. They must be defeated, by all measures at our disposal. My family has supported the Reaper since before he was known. My brother died for him. I have fought for him. And I will not abandon him now. Nor should you. The Optimates stand with the Reaper. And we propose a bill to the floor for a Resolution of Liberty Eternal, to draft twenty million fresh troops, to allocate ships from the Gulf, and to levy additional taxes to fund the war effort until the Core is free." Daxo sits back down and makes a pained expression in my direction and rubs his temple.

Publius cu Caraval rises from his seat when the applause finally fades. His short copper hair is parted on the side, not a strand out of place. "I was told I was brought into this world to serve. To move the invisible levers of an ancient and evil machine. We all moved those levers. But now we serve the People. We are here to liberate the dignity of man. Darrow of Lykos is our greatest weapon against tyranny. Let us sharpen him again so he can break the chains for our brothers and sisters in bondage on Venus." He touches his heart, bleeding empathy and resolution.

A chorus of senators declare their support, each shouting over the next. Mustang stands, hammering down her Dawn Scepter. "The resolution is registered by the Senate and now open for debate."

All eyes turn to Dancer.

He has not yet moved. Mustang analyzes his face. "Senator O'Faran," she says. "Nothing?"

"Thank you, my Sovereign." He picks at the edges of his toga in his nervous habit before rising to his feet. To this day he loathes public speaking. His voice is hoarse and halting, as far from Publius's as possible. "ArchImperator, my friend, my brother, can I first begin by saying how happy I am to have you home. There is no . . . greater son of the Republic." Many heads nod. "I would also like to personally offer you congratulations on the *partial* liberation of Mercury. Despite your methods, which I will get to in a spit."

I watch him warily, knowing what he intends, but not how it's meant to be delivered.

"You all know I am a man of war." He looks at his rough hands. "I have held weapons. I have led men. It's what I am. And like most of you, I am also a mortal in a war of giants." He looks at the Golds, the Obsidians. "But I have learned that giants can be felled with words. Words are our . . . salvation. So I stand here before you armed only with that voice." He pauses, grimacing to himself. "And I want to ask you, what age do you want to live in? One where the sword leads and we follow? Or an age where our voice can sing louder than an engine can roar? Was that not the Song of Persephone? The dream of Eo of Lykos?"

There are murmurs of agreement from his supporters.

An inner bitterness wells as he insinuates my deviation from Eo's dream. She was mine and I lost her to them. But each time she's mentioned, even in reverence, it seems to me as though she's been dug from the ground and paraded for the crowd.

"Senators, we have no power in and of ourselves," Dancer continues slowly. "We are just vessels. Men and women chosen to speak for the People, by the People, to channel their voice to protect the People. Darrow, you helped give the People a voice. For that, we are in your debt.

"But now you refuse to listen to that voice, to obey the laws you helped make. You were given an order by the Senate, by the People, to stand down over Mercury. You disobeyed that order. You released an Iron Rain." He looks to Sefi. She sits several seats down from Sevro on the guest benches, watching with an unreadable expression. "Because of your impatience, a million of our brothers and sisters died in a single day. Two hundred thousand Obsidians. *Two hundred thousand.* A number that cannot be replaced." The words are heavy as they fall, and I see the solemn anger of the Obsidian bloc, the same anger I've felt from Sefi since that day. "Not only did you do this, but you illegally pillaged elements of the Fourth Fleet that guards Mars to add to your assault on Mercury. Why?"

"Because it was necessary to—"

"One million souls."

I knew thirty-seven of those souls, and somehow that number seems larger than one million. "A man once said that a war fought by politicians will be lost by everyone," I say bitterly. "Harnassus and Orion supported my plan. Your legions have protected you this far. But now you question them?"

"Our legions?" he asks. "Are they ours?" Before I can answer, he lumbers forward, wrangling control of the conversation with all the grace of an old bear.

"How many of us have lost loved ones to war? How many of us have buried sons, daughters, wives, husbands? My hands are raw from digging graves. My heart shatters seeing genocide and starvation on planets we claim free. On Mars, my home. How many more must suffer to free Mercury and Venus, planets now so indoctrinated that our own Colors will fight against us for every inch of ground we take?"

"So as long as Mars is free, you're content to call it a day? Leave the others to rot?" I ask.

He looks me in the eyes. "Is Mars free? Ask a Red from the mines. Ask a Pink in Agea's ghetto. The yoke of poverty is as heavy as that of tyranny."

Mustang interjects. "We have a solemn duty to rid the worlds of the stain of slavery. Your own words, Senator."

"We also have a solemn duty to make those worlds better than they were before," Dancer replies. "Two hundred million have died since House Lune fell. Tell me, what is the purpose of victory if it destroys us? If we are stretched so thin that we cannot protect or provide for those we bring out of the mines?"

There are no weapons in the room, save those of Wulfgar and his Warden, but Dancer's words do damage enough. They rattle the Senate hall. And he's not finished.

"Darrow, you stand here asking us for more men and women, more ships to wage this war. So I ask you, and pray to the Old Man who guards the Vale that you can give me an answer, when will this war end?"

"When the Republic is safe."

"Will it be safe when the Ash Lord falls? When we have Venus?"

"The Ash Lord is the heart of their war machine. But he rules with fear. Without him, the remaining Gold houses will turn on each other within a week."

"And what of the Rim? What if they come and we've smashed our armies to bits to kill one man?"

"We have a peace treaty with the Rim."

"For now."

"Their docks are destroyed. Octavia saw to that. The Starhall analysts believe they could not attack us, even if they wanted to, for another fifteen years," Mustang says.

"Romulus does not want another war," I say. "Trust me on that."

"Trust you?" My old friend frowns. "We have trusted you, Darrow." I feel the same anger in him that I saw when he learned of what I did to the Sons on the Rim. "So many have trusted you. For so many years. But you're in love with your own myth. You think that the Reaper knows better than the People."

"You think I want war? I loathe it. It's stolen my friends. My family. It takes me away from my wife. From my child. If there were another path, I would take it. But there is no path around this war. The only way is *through*."

He watches me for a moment.

"I wonder, would you even know peace if you saw it?" He turns to the senators. "What if I told you, what if I told all of you there *was* another path? One that has been hidden from us?" Caraval frowns and leans forward. Sevro glances my way. "What if we could have safety not tomorrow, not a decade from now. But right this very moment? Peace without another Iron Rain. Without throwing millions more into the guns of the Ash Lord?" He turns to my wife. "My Sovereign, I invoke my right to present a witness to the Senate body."

She's caught off guard. "What witness?"

Dancer does not answer. He looks expectantly down the corridor to his right. At the end of it, a door opens and a lone set of heels click against the stone floor. In hushed silence, the senators crane their necks to see a tall, imperious woman of later years striding out of the corridor into the Senate hall. She stands a head taller than the Republic Wardens, excepting Wulfgar, as she passes on the way to the center of the floor. Her eyes are Gold. Her body serene and slight, despite her height. Her hair is spun behind her and caged by gold mesh. A gold collar in the shape of an eagle encloses her neck. Her gown is black and covering every bit of skin from her neck to her toes. And upon her regal, bitter face is a single curved scar.

I glare at the woman. She has been shadow to my life ever since I beat her favorite son to death in a simple stone room sixteen years ago. Now she comes to stand before the Senate.

"What is the meaning of this?" Mustang demands, rising from her chair to dominate the room. Dancer does not back down.

"This is Julia au Bellona," he says against the rising furor. "She brings a message from the Ash Lord."

"Senator . . ." Anger flushes Mustang's face, and she takes a violent step forward. "That is not your place! Foreign diplomacy is the province of the Sovereign! You overstep."

"So does your husband, but do you scold him?" he asks. "Hear what she has to say. You will find it illuminating." The senators shout their desire to hear Bellona out. Dread enters me. I know what Julia will say.

Mustang is trapped. She looks down at the woman, both the remnants of two great Gold houses that destroyed one another in their feud. Of their families, only Cassius remains. If he is still alive somewhere out there. "Say your piece, Bellona."

Julia looks up at Mustang with utmost distaste. She's not forgotten how Mustang sat at their table with Cassius and then turned her back on them.

“Usurper,” she says, refusing to use Mustang’s honorific. Her eyes look upon the senators with aristocratic disdain. “I traveled a month to stand before you. I will speak plainly so you understand. The Ash Lord tires of war. Of seeing cities turned to rubble.” She continues over shouts of protest. “During the Siege of Mercury, emissaries, including myself, were sent to the *Morning Star* to seek audience with your . . . warlord.” She glares at me. “We asked for an armistice. He replied with an Iron Rain.”

“Armistice?” Mustang murmurs.

“And why did you request an armistice?” Dancer prompts over the whispering senators.

“The Ash Lord, and the War Council of the Society, wish to discuss terms. . . .”

“What terms?” Dancer presses. “Speak plainly, Gold.”

“Did the Reaper not tell you?” She looks at me and smiles. “We requested a cease-fire in order to discuss the terms of a permanent and lasting peace between the Rising and the Society.”

11

DARROW

Servant of the People

THE ROOM BURSTS INTO A CHAOS of thrust fists and rippling togas. Only the Obsidians do not move. Sefi watches the reaction with a neutral expression, unreadable as ever. Mustang turns on me in a fury. "Is this true?"

"He never wanted peace," I say coldly. Sevro is rocking in his seat in an effort to keep himself from strangling Julia au Bellona in the middle of the Forum.

"But he did send emissaries?"

"He sent provocateurs. Her and Asmodeus. It was a ruse that I did not warrant worth the time of this body."

Mustang can't believe what she's hearing. "Darrow . . ."

"Asmodeus was on your ship and you did not report this to us?" Dancer asks, incredulous. Someone betrayed me. Someone in the Howlers. How else would he know? "Next you'll say the Fear Knight himself was in your mess hall."

I fix my gaze on Dancer. "The Ash Lord burned Rhea. He burned New Thebes. He'd burn every city left to win back Luna. He wants the home we've stolen from him."

Dancer shakes his head. "You had no right."

Caraval and those Coppers who cheered me watch with uncertainty. Mustang has not moved from her chair, nor can she. Whatever she says will be dismissed as a wife defending her husband and might indict her as well. If they think she knew, she'll be impeached, possibly worse. Which is the very reason why I hid this from her.

My star is falling. If she holds on, it will drag her down too. Better to stay quiet, my love. Better to play the long game. I know better than to struggle. A Red senator lurches up from her seat and rushes across the floor. For a moment, I think she means to speak in my defense. Then she spits at my feet. "Gold," she says. Wulfgar eases forward to dissuade any others from breaking protocol.

For years I waited for this day to come, but as the Republic grew in strength, it never did. And I suppose I tricked myself into thinking it wouldn't. But now that it's here, now that I feel the blind hate rising and see the unpitying lenses of the cameras in the viewing deck above, I know how words will be lost on them. The noble newscasters will sanctimoniously peel at every decision, every secret, every sin, and stream them across the worlds, feigning duty, but delighting in the moral bloodshed, masticating my bones, cracking them for the marrow of ratings and feeding their vulture appetite for gossip.

I'm not surprised, but I am heartbroken. I don't want to be the villain. Wulfgar looks back at me pityingly, as if wishing he could carry me away from this public shaming. Sevro is standing from his seat in a rage.

"You fucking backstabbing little rat . . ." he says to Dancer.

"How can we trust you with our armies," Dancer booms, "when you disobey the Senate? When you lie to the People?" He does not give me time to respond. "My brothers and sisters, there is no place in our Republic for warlords or tyrants. They are the death of demokracy. Our seven hundred years of slavery stands testament to that! But tyranny did not just spring up. It bubbled up slowly, as the leaders of Earth watched and did nothing. We must choose. Is our Republic ruled by its voice, or by its sword?"

He sits, his work done. Amidst a roar of approval that spreads to more than just his usual supporters, Dancer of Faran, the hand of Ares who pulled me from the grave to make me a weapon, buries me under my own designs. And across the room, like a noble old olive tree neither flame nor axe can fell, Julia au Bellona watches me with hate in her gnawing eyes. Slowly, as if a long-forgotten promise is finally being delivered, she begins to smile.

Publius cu Caraval stands in the chaos. Only by Mustang hammering her scepter on the ground can she quiet the senators enough for the Copper to speak. If anyone could find something to say to defend me, it would be him.

"I do not share all the convictions of the Red senator. There cannot be peace while there is no justice. But in one matter, I fear he strikes the mark. You have overstepped, ArchImperator. You have forgotten your oaths made to serve the People." He turns to the senators, summoning firm courage to overcome the betrayal. "I propose a vote to remove Darrow of Lykos from high command and to place him under house arrest pending a trial for acts of treason against the Republic." Applause follows this. He looks back at me dramatically. "And I propose a temporary cessation of hostilities with the Golds of the Core so that we may decide ourselves between war and peace."

The sanctimonious bastard.

There is little Mustang can do. At her instructions, Republic Wardens come to escort all non-senators from the room. I let Wulfgar guide me out. Over the heads of his men, I see my wife watching me from her chair, fear in her eyes because she sees the rage in mine.

Outside the building, the world is quiet and untouched by my humiliation. Republic Wardens stand illuminated by the warm glow of blue lamps as we collect our weapons. Lesser bureaucrats thread their way across the plaza, tending to the affairs of a government responsible for ten billion lives. Dusk is over now and the sky is black. Autumn leaves roll across the white marble expanse.

"Darrow, you are not to leave the city," Wulfgar says to me. "Do you hear me?" He puts his hand on my shoulder again. "Darrow . . ."

"Am I under arrest?" I ask.

"Not yet . . ."

"You need to step back," Sevro says, his fingers tightening around the razor at his side. Wulfgar looks down at Sevro, who comes barely to his sternum, and steps back in respect. I descend the stairs away from the Forum, heading for the landing pads in the North Citadel. Sevro catches up to me. I stop and look back at the Forum as a loud cheer leaks out the open door.

"Some little shit told them," Sevro says. "I should carve Caraval's balls off. Treason? They can't actually arrest you, can they?"

"They might not put me in Deepgrave, but they'll lock me up for as long as they think they don't need me. Long enough for the Ash Lord to make his move."

Sevro sneers. "The Seventh Legion will have something to say about that. Should I call Orion? The Telemanuses? Kavax should be on his way back from Mars. . . ."

I look back to the Forum. Inside, Mustang will be attempting to repair the damage done. But with Copper lost, she won't have the votes to protect me. There's nothing more I can do here. This isn't my world. I knew it before, and Dancer just reminded me. The man says all I know is war. And he is right. In my heart, I know my enemy. I know his mettle. I know his cruelty. And I know this war will not end with politicians smiling at each other from across a table.

It will only end as it began: with blood.

"No, Sevro. Summon the Howlers."

PHOTO: © JOAN ALLEN

PIERCE BROWN is the #1 *New York Times* bestselling author of *Red Rising*, *Golden Son*, *Morning Star*, *Iron Gold*, *Dark Age*, and *Light Bringer*. His work has been published in thirty-four languages and thirty-six territories. He lives in Los Angeles, where he is at work on his next novel.

piercebrown.com
Facebook.com/PierceBrownAuthor
Twitter: @Pierce_Brown
Instagram: @PierceBrownOfficial

To inquire about booking Pierce Brown for a speaking engagement, please contact the Penguin Random House Speakers Bureau at speakers@penguinrandomhouse.com.

THE RED RISING SAGA CONTINUES

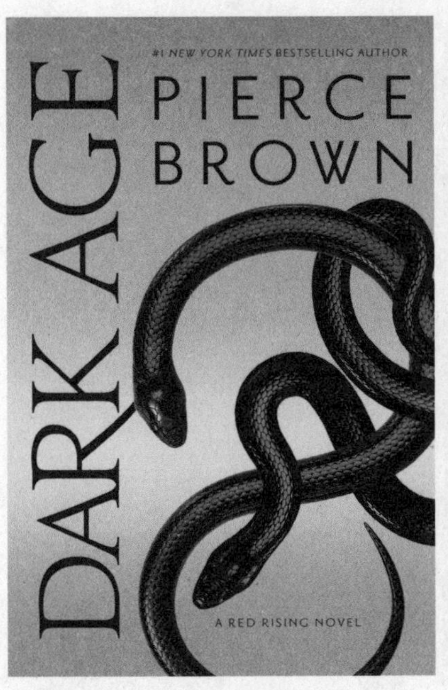